Ernest Arthur Gardner

Naukratis

Part II

Ernest Arthur Gardner

Naukratis
Part II

ISBN/EAN: 9783742840479

Manufactured in Europe, USA, Canada, Australia, Japa

Cover: Foto ©Andreas Hilbeck / pixelio.de

Manufactured and distributed by brebook publishing software
(www.brebook.com)

Ernest Arthur Gardner

Naukratis

NAUKRATIS.

PART II.

ERNEST A. GARDNER, M.A.,

FELLOW OF GONVILLE AND CAIUS COLLEGE, CRAVEN STUDENT AND FORMERLY WORTS STUDENT OF THE UNIVERSITY OF CAMBRIDGE ;
DIRECTOR OF THE BRITISH SCHOOL OF ARCHÆOLOGY AT ATHENS.

WITH AN APPENDIX,

BY

F. LL. GRIFFITH, B.A.,

OF THE BRITISH MUSEUM, FORMERLY STUDENT OF THE EGYPT EXPLORATION FUND.

SIXTH MEMOIR OF

THE EGYPT EXPLORATION FUND.

PUBLISHED BY ORDER OF THE COMMITTEE.

TRÜBNER & CO., 57 & 59, LUDGATE HILL, E.C.

1888.

LONDON:
PRINTED BY GILBERT AND RIVINGTON, LIMITED,
ST. JOHN'S HOUSE, CLERKENWELL ROAD.

W. M. FLINDERS PETRIE.

Οὔνομα σὸν μακαριστὸν, ὃ Ναύκρατις ὧδε φυλάζει
ἔστ᾽ ἂν ἴῃ Νείλου ναῦς ἔφαλος τεναγη.

Posidippus ap. Ath. 318 D.

PREFACE.

When a work begun by one hand is continued by another, an explanation or apology seems to be required. I trust however that in the present case some degree of continuity may be found in the reports of the excavations we have conducted at Naukratis for the Egypt Exploration Fund. For I was by Mr. Petrie's kindness enabled to study the yet unpublished results of his first season's exploration, and to have my conclusions incorporated in his report; and the excavations of the subsequent season were begun under his direction and after his system. The present volume also contains some of his handiwork, in the plates signed with his initials and the description of the articles contained therein. But above all, both in the introductory narrative and in the dedication I have endeavoured to show my sense of obligation to one whose discoveries have led to the results recorded in this volume as well as in Naukratis vol. I.

Mr. Griffith also was with us for a short time at Naukratis. The results of his special work will be found in the Appendix of this volume, and in the plate which he has drawn (XXIV.). For another plate (XXIII.) we are indebted to the kindness of Mme. Naville.

In preparing the plans of the temples, I have met with the greatest assistance from Professor Middleton, by whose advice I have given them theform in which they now are seen. The general plan (Pl. IV.) is reduced from one made by Mr. Chapman of the Fitzwilliam Museum, which was based upon Mr. Petrie's plan, with such modifications and additions as our later excavations had rendered necessary.

The photographic plates have been executed under my supervision by Mr. Griggs ; as they are collotyped directly from photographs of the originals, their accuracy may be relied upon.

I have in the narrative of our season's work referred to the help and kindness with which I have met on every side during my stay in Egypt; it is my pleasing duty to acknowledge especially the consideration I received from Mr. Maspéro and others holding official positions in Egypt, and from Dr. R. S. Poole and other officers of the Egypt Exploration Fund in England.

To the University of Cambridge I am indebted for the grant from the Worts Fund which enabled me to undertake the excavations in Egypt. I have therefore to lay before the University the present memoir as a report of the work for which it equipped me.

Last, but not least, I would acknowledge my obligations to my brother, Professor Percy Gardner of Oxford. To him I owe alike my first impulse to the study of archæology and the first suggestion of the particular piece of excavation of which this volume is the record. I have also been indebted to him for advice and assistance both during my work in Egypt and during my preparation of its results for publication. I therefore feel that his name fittingly concludes the list of acknowledgments with which I would preface this book.

ERNEST ARTHUR GARDNER.

CAMBRIDGE, 1888.

CONTENTS.

a

LIST OF PLATES.

NAUKRATIS.

PART II.

CHAPTER I.

(1) The discovery of Naukratis and the first season's work upon its site have already been described by Mr. Petrie. But before we enter upon the description of another year's excavations, it seems advisable to pause for a moment, and to realize what was already accomplished when Mr. Petrie left Egypt in the summer of 1885, what still remained to be unearthed by a continuation of his successful labours.

In forming such an estimate of the results of exploration on an ancient site, it is well to compare the scholar's expectations, based upon literature and history, with the material and tangible attainments of the spade. And at Naukratis it is both easy and useful to carry out this comparison. For the literary evidence, if not very extensive, is clear and definite; and in the process of excavation a fortunate profusion of testimony, and especially the testimony of inscriptions, has removed from the sphere of discussion or doubt the identification of the various sites and buildings that have come to light.

From ancient literature we know of five early religious foundations at Naukratis; four of these are mentioned by Herodotus: first the Great Hellenion, then the precincts separately dedicated by the Æginetans to Zeus, by the Samians to Hera, and by the Milesians to Apollo. Of a fifth foundation, apparently as early and as important as any of these, we hear from Athenæus, who tells a story, to which we shall have to recur, about the favour shown by Aphrodite to a Naukratite in danger at sea, and about a Cypriote image dedicated by him to the goddess in her temple at Naukratis.

Now of these five temples or sacred enclosures, two, the Hellenion and that dedicated by the Milesians to Apollo, were found by Mr. Petrie in his first year's excavations. One or two fragments of inscribed vases had given reason to hope that two more, those of Aphrodite and Hera, might also come to light; but no definite conclusions as to their exact sites or identification were possible. Another temenous, not mentioned by classical authors, was also discovered, and was proved by the evidence of inscriptions to be sacred to the Dioscuri; but their temple still remained buried. Mr. Petrie had also produced a most careful and elaborate plan, not only of the sites on which he had worked, but of all the streets of the ancient city, so far as it was possible to trace them.

(2) Such was the state in which Mr. Petrie

B

loft the excavations, after his discovery of the city of Naukratis, and his first season's work upon its site. Obviously there was every prospect of good results if that work should be continued. But Mr. Petrie, in his characteristic and disinterested zeal for new discoveries, was anxious to proceed to new fields, if he could find any one to carry on the work he had begun, and to gather in the results of his previous attainments. It was accordingly arranged that I should accompany him to Naukratis at the beginning of the next season; and that Mr. Petrie himself, when he had started the work and stayed with me long enough to enable me to become familiar with the methods that he had adopted, should again pursue his quest of new sites and unexplored regions. The success that has again attended his search is already known to all: it remains for me to give some account of the continuation of his work at Naukratis, both while he was able to superintend it in person, and after he had left it in my charge.

(3) In accordance with the arrangement above mentioned, I accompanied Mr. Petrie to Egypt at the end of November, 1885; and after we had obtained our papers from the government, and engaged our raises or overseers, we proceeded to Naukratis. There, after a few days, we were joined by Mr. Griffith. We were fortunate in being able to hire for the season the whole of the house—or palace—in which Mr. Petrie and Mr. Griffith had in the previous season occupied a few rooms only. This afterwards proved to be a most convenient acquisition, as it allowed ample storage-room for the numerous antiquities that had to be safely housed.

We found the site of the city already somewhat altered by the destructive operations of the Arabs, who are continually carrying off the earth from ancient sites to spread it upon their fields. In this way the walls of the Great Temenos or Hellenion had almost disappeared, and the appearance of the mound that takes the place of the ancient city had in several respects been altered. But though, on the one hand, this process is destructive, it is also, on the other, of great service to the excavator, for the digging of the Arabs is constantly laying bare new strata and disclosing new sites, and a careful watching of their work and the objects they find will often supply far more information than large and numerous trial pits or trenches.

(4) After we had taken a general survey of the city, and resolved upon the spots which seemed most promising either for thorough exploration or for testing by trial trenches, we at once set to work. At first we had only a few workmen, but their number quickly increased, till some 200 were in our employ.[1] As many as this were kept in the work while Mr. Petrie was still with me; after he had left I found 120 to 150 was as large a number as I alone could keep under proper supervision. For though our overseers were excellently trained by Mr. Petrie, and thoroughly trustworthy, it was of course most undesirable to leave any site where excavation was going on for many hours without a visit. At first, however, as there were three of us to direct the labourers, we were able to make a division of the work. Mr. Petrie, while keeping in his hands the general direction of our plans, devoted himself more especially to arranging and watching the large trial trenches, by which he was testing various interesting parts of the mound. Mr. Griffith paid special attention to the work that was being done in carefully clearing ascertained sites within the ancient city; and I directed the workmen who dug

_____

[1] The numbers, here and elsewhere, include the boys and girls who carried baskets, as well as the men who worked with the mattock.

some trial pits in the low mounds to the north, where we hoped to find the ancient cemetery, and superintended the excavation of the tombs after our search had proved successful. But though we thus undertook respectively the responsibility of some portion of the excavation, our work was really done in common, or at least in consultation with one another.

(5) The first work attempted and the first result gained was in the enclosure which Mr. Petrie had in the previous season identified as the temen s of the Dioscuri. Here, after a very little earth had been removed, some oblong structures of mud-brick were found. These were faced with plaster; indeed, it was the plaster facing that led to their discovery, for without such a facing it is often very difficult, if not impossible, to tell a wall of unbaked mud-brick from the hardened mud that surrounds it. It soon became evident that these structures had been either the bases of pillars, or the lower portion of those pillars themselves. Thus we had the portico in the front of a small temple, facing westwards, as might be expected in the case of a temple dedicated to heroes, and not to a god. After three weeks of excavation, the site of this temple was completely cleared; but only the northern wall of its cella could be found in addition to the pillars at first discovered; a few fragments of vases, some inscribed with dedications to the Dioscuri, also came to light.

(6) The next site to be found was that of the cemetery of the ancient town. It has already been mentioned that we determined to look for this in the low mounds that lie to the north of Naukratis; one of them is covered by a modern Arab village; but another smaller one was unoccupied, and offered a convenient opportunity for excavation. Three trenches were cut across it, and in a few hours the middle trench came upon a tile coffin. The

coffin contained nothing except some traces of bones; but more coffins and other indications soon proved that we had found the object of our search. Accordingly all the men were drawn into a line, and a deep trench, descending to the water level, was dug along the whole length of one side of the mound. When completed, the trench was made gradually to advance across the mound, so that the whole of the contents of this portion of the cemetery were turned over—a process which occupied sixty work-people for about ten weeks. Of the graves and their contents I shall have to speak in a subsequent chapter, but it is as well to say at once that the results of this search have been rather disappointing. It is at least clear that only a portion of the cemetery of Naukratis has been exhumed—and that portion one which dates from a later time, when the city had already passed its most flourishing periods. Some trial pits were also sunk on unoccupied bits of ground in the village, between the small mound to the north and the ancient city itself; these served to show that the cemetery also underlies this village, but the tombs actually found were precisely similar, both in age and character, to those discovered in the smaller mound. However, it seems a probable supposition that the earliest and most interesting part of the ancient cemetery of Naukratis still lies buried beneath the Arab village. But in the heavy mud soil of the Delta it is not to be hoped that any vases or other breakable objects could be recovered in a complete or uninjured condition.

(7) Next, in order of time, though not in order of importance, comes the most interesting and fruitful discovery of the season—the temple of Aphrodite. The story told by Athenæus, and already referred to, is of a nature to give us a peculiar interest in this temple and its contents; and last season some fragments of pottery bearing dedications to the

goddess had been found not far from the region in which her temple and precinct were ultimately identified. Accordingly numerous large trenches were dug in the neighbourhood of the place where these inscriptions had been found; but though one of these trenches actually cut into the temenos wall, within a yard or two of the temple itself, it was not by such means that the temple was actually found. Thus an excellent illustration was afforded of the comparative uselessness of extensive trial trenches upon such a site. The sides of a trench usually present a uniform black surface; and even if a few courses of mud-brick are here and there distinguishable, it is by no means easy to infer the size and direction of the wall of which they form a part. The ultimate discovery was, as has been already said, made by other means. Some men, digging on their own account, close to the end of our trench, came by chance upon a number of fragments of pottery with incised and painted dedications to Aphrodite. Here at last it was clear that we were in the immediate neighbourhood of the temple; the particular spot afterwards proved to be within the temenos, just to the north of the temple itself. This building was identified without much trouble after a careful examination of the site. It had been already observed by Mr. Petrie in the previous season, and marked upon his plan; but a deceptive appearance of a door in one corner had prevented his recognizing its true arrangement and purport. As soon as the identification had been made, all the loose rubbish on the surface was cleared away from the temple and its neighbourhood. Thereupon an oblong structure emerged in front of the face of the temple towards the east. The corner of this structure had been visible before, but no more. It consisted of thin mud-brick walls, faced with plaster. From its position, the conjecture was obvious that this was the great

altar of burnt offering—a conjecture soon changed to a certainty by the discovery of ashes and fragments of bone within the structure, and of steps leading up to it from the temple. But it is perhaps worth while to record a doubt which at first arose, as the possibility of such a doubt is an illustration of the difficulty of distinguishing unburnt brick from mud. It was for a while hard to decide whether the brick, to which the plaster served as a facing, lay within the plaster, or without it, whether the coat of plaster served to cover the inside of the walls of a small chamber, or the outside of a more or less solid structure. Then within the temple itself a wall was found dividing the cella from the opisthodomus. But more than this, it was clear that the divisional wall, and the lower part of the main walls of the temple, which were partly faced with plaster, belonged to an earlier building than the one which was at first visible; these earlier walls had clearly served as a foundation on which the later ones, which we had at first seen, were built; and the floor of the latest temple must have been at the level where the earlier walls ceased. When, however, the level of the altar came to be considered, its top was found to be on a level with the floor of the earlier of the two temples we had already found; and its base was some six or seven feet lower. Now there was no reason for assuming any previous inequality in the level of the ground; hence it was probable that the altar must belong to a building of much earlier date, which was buried to a considerable depth before even the earlier of the other two temples was begun. Of this earliest temple the walls soon came to light in the course of excavation; they had served as a foundation, on which the walls of the second temple had been built, just as those other walls had, in their turn, supported a later structure. Thus was found the plan of three temples of very different dates; the details of the differences between the three must be reserved for a special chapter. Of course all these discoveries were not made at once; though some indications quickly appeared, three months elapsed before the earliest temple and its precinct were completely cleared. One of the earliest trenches, however, sunk to the north of the temple, aroused expectations which were afterwards fully realized; deep in the earth was found a very rich stratum of fragments of the finest painted and inscribed vases. But in order to reach these without fear of damaging them, of course the plan of sinking narrow trenches had to be given up, and the whole earth was gradually removed in horizontal layers. Thus it was possible to ascertain exactly the level of everything found, and also to extract carefully delicate or breakable objects; but such a process necessarily caused a long delay before the rich layer of fragments could be reached.

(8) Meanwhile work in other parts of the town was progressing. Another fortunate chance led us to the discovery of an important site. A stone was offered us bearing an inscription (ἱερὸν Διὸς Ἀποτροπαίου), which seemed to denote that the place it came from was sacred. Accordingly we ascertained from the finder the exact spot where it had been discovered, and began an investigation of the neighbourhood. This proved to be within the large enclosure called the Palæstra by Mr. Petrie last year. Very soon one or two fragments dedicated to Hera were found. Then the work was left for a while; when it was resumed some two months afterwards, a few more such dedications and the foundation of a building were found—enough to prove that this enclosure was the temenos once dedicated by the Samians to Hera, and that one of the most promising sites in Naukratis had nothing left to reward the excavator except its name. Here was a case in which the digging of the

Arabs had proved most disastrous. The temple had been of stone; therefore all of it, except one or two insignificant fragments which were recovered, had been carried off: and the actual digging had reached right down to the original ground level of the ancient town, in some places even below it. Of course all antiquities found in this process had been thrown away or destroyed. A few fragments were found among the heaps of potsherds and other refuse that had been left behind; but it was from a few bits of undisturbed earth that there came the best and clearest specimens of dedications to Hera. This fact seems to prove that these dedications really belong to the site upon which they were discovered, and have not wandered there by chance from any other region.

(9) Thus we had, in the first few weeks of our stay, discovered two more of the most important temples at Naukratis, whose existence was known from the evidence of literature: but it was not to be expected that our search would in every case prove equally fortunate. Large and deep trial trenches were sunk in various parts of the ancient town which looked promising, and which had not yet been tested. From these not very much further result was obtained; but the chief discoveries made by their means were at opposite ends of the town, one on the N.E. corner of the mound, the other between the Hellenion and the canal.

(10) In this latter place it seemed probable that a great road or avenue must have existed, to serve as an approach from the quay to the principal sanctuary of the city. A broad and long trench was made along the probable direction of this avenue; and in it was found the lower part of a granite sphinx, of the Ptolemaic period. The sphinx had been split up, in order that the stone might be used for other purposes; even on the part left wedge-holes could be seen, intended to serve for splitting off

another portion. But this destruction must have taken place at some remote period, for the sphinx was about six feet below the present level of the ground. By a later search two large portions that had been broken off were recovered, and then were restored to their original position—not without some difficulty, for they could only just be lifted by six or seven men. Thus the whole sphinx again stood complete, with the exception of the face only, which could not be found.

(11) The discoveries made by means of the trial trenches at the N.E. of the mound were less definite and comprehensible. A large wall was found, which for a while we supposed to be the enclosing wall of the city itself: connected with this were various large and very solid buildings, constructed partly of mud-brick, partly of stone; the latter material had of course disappeared, leaving only its foundations to be traced. The purpose or use of these buildings could not be conjectured either from their plan or from the objects found in them; but they did not appear to date from a time before the Ptolemaic period.

(12) Almost all the excavations already referred to were begun within the first three weeks after our arrival: in order to avoid confusion, I have in many cases stated at once facts which did not become clear till weeks or months more had elapsed. Mr. Petrie left Naukratis to proceed to other work, farther to the east, on the 5th of January, 1886; Mr. Griffith had also gone a few days earlier. I accordingly assumed the charge of the work, and continued it for the next three months. For a week (11—18 January), I was fortunate in having the valuable help of Mr. A. H. Smith, who especially devoted himself to watching the work at the cemetery during that time; and I was very sorry that his health prevented him from making a longer stay. For the rest of the season I was alone at Naukratis; and I

found my time and attention very fully occupied with the excavation of the various sites I have already mentioned. I endeavoured as far as possible never to have my work on more than two important sites at a time, in order that I might be able both to watch it constantly myself, and to keep it under the eyes of my two excellent and trustworthy overseers, Mahajub and Said Abu Daud. Of course many smaller outlying pieces of digging had to be done; but these were, as a rule, carried out by contract work. The temple of the Dioscuri was finished in the beginning of January; for the next two months the temple of Aphrodite and the cemetery formed the two chief centres of excavation; later the temples of Aphrodite and of Hera.

(13) The chief feature of the work during the whole of these months was the richness of the temple of Aphrodite and its precinct. I have already referred to the layer of fragments whose existence we had ascertained, but which had to be approached gradually. Even before the level was reached at which these fragments had previously been found, numerous pieces of pottery and statuettes made their appearance; and that too not only on the north side of the temple, but also on the east and on the south. Here was no trench like that in which Mr. Petrie had in the first season found the bowls discarded from the service of the Milesian Apollo, but a continuous layer of refuse, bounded only by the walls of the temenos itself, and sometimes even scattered beyond them. How this refuse came into the position where it was found is, and must remain, a matter of conjecture; but it is hard to believe that any event in the peaceful administration of the temple could have produced such a result. It seems hardly rash in this connexion to think of the disturbances which accompanied the Persian invasion of Egypt, especially as the period preceding that invasion would well suit the style and character of the various vases and

statuettes that have been recovered. Nor is the consistency of the layer of refuse other than one might expect to have been formed if the temple were destroyed by violence. It was made up of the fragments of hundreds, or even thousands of vases, all mixed up together in the utmost confusion, and of numerous archaic statuettes, or fragments of statuettes. Evidently these had all been votive offerings in the temple of Aphrodite, as was indeed attested by the dedications with which many of them were described. Mingled with them here and there were ashes or pieces of bone. Such was the extent and richness of this layer, that even after we had gradually cleared off the earth from above it, and left it free to be worked, nearly two months elapsed before the whole of it could be gathered in. Meanwhile, my resources for storing this great quantity, and keeping the product of different parts separate, were somewhat strained. At first we had attempted to keep all the fragments which we found in paper bags, which had been provided by the foresight of Mr. Petrie ; thus each bag could be labelled, and the sites distinguished by an easy system of numbering. But this manner of proceeding soon proved inadequate ; then the baskets used for carrying the earth in digging were pressed into the service, and the number of these baskets of potsherds brought in every day came to be considerable ; on one day there were nine, on several seven, from four to six on others. Thus it was easy to bring the fragments in separate baskets up to the house, and there they were emptied, at first, into boxes devoted to various portions of the site. Soon all my boxes were filled, and then I felt the benefit of the space at my disposal, for I was able to devote one room to the reception of these potsherds, and to partition off its floor in such a way as to keep the various piles distinct. After the first few days, it also became impossible to sort, or even select these fragments as they came in. This is obvious, when one considers that sometimes perhaps as many as 5000 potsherds were found in a single day, and the work of sorting and selecting can be properly done only by daylight. I accordingly had to content myself with glancing through the contents of each basket, to make sure that it really consisted of painted fragments of vases, and had no rubbish put in to fill up. Though I afterwards rejected a certain amount, I was obliged to wait till I had worked through the whole in England, before making a final selection. For if I had at random thrown away any pieces that seemed in themselves unimportant, I should have run the risk of spoiling the completeness of a vase whose other fragments had been recovered. If I had kept too much, the mistake admitted of an easy remedy ; it was not so if I had kept too little.

(14) Towards the end of the season, when work was slackening a little on the site of the ancient city, I managed to make trial of a spot of which Mr. Petrie entertained some hopes. It seemed not improbable that we might there find another and an earlier part of the old cemetery. This was on the mound of Neqrash, a village which, as Mr. Griffith [1] has pointed out, still preserves the name of Naukratis itself. It is situated about a mile away towards the east. Here I sank several large and deep pits, but I found nothing whatever, except a bit of wall in one place, apparently of the Ptolemaic period. This at least proves that here there was no cemetery like the one we found on the north of the city ; for there the graves were so closely packed that even very small trenches were sure to find something, and those I made at Neqrash were of considerable dimensions.

(15) Another and an even more promising attempt met with an equally disappointing result. At different times during the season, as occasion offered, various private dwelling

---

[1] See page 80.

houses in the ancient town were cleared. But whether because this attempt is not of much use on such a site, or because the houses were unfortunately chosen, very little was gained by the clearance. Of one house, indeed, a plan was recovered, but as there were no doors whatever, it was clearly only a basement or cellar plan, and though something might be inferred from the walls as to the position of the dwelling rooms above, none of this upper portion was left standing. In other cases even less success was attained. One or two houses look very promising to the excavator in the conjectural restoration of their arrangement, given in the plan made in the preceding season by Mr. Petrie. This plan was made with the help of various indications, such as small extant bits of wall and the like. And as these bits of wall still stood up amidst the wilderness of rough or late pottery, it was natural to suppose that if their base were cleared the system of which they formed a part would at once become apparent. But this was not the case; when the excavation had been carried down to the most ancient level of the ground, the arrangement of the houses remained as much a matter of conjecture as before. And very little in the way of antiquities was found during this work. Doubtless the houses, built entirely of mud-brick, had gradually subsided and served as a foundation for the buildings of a later generation : and in this way little either of the walls themselves or of the objects they once contained remains to be found by excavation.

(16) But on such a site as that of Naukratis the explorer does not rely only upon the workmen in his employ and under his direction for the discovery either of sites or of antiquities. Mention has already been made of a practice of the natives of the Delta which is of the highest importance to archæologists, both for what it brings to light and for what it destroys. But for this practice the site of Naukratis would not yet have been discovered; yet it must have led to the destruction of many valuable and interesting objects that would else be still safely hidden under twenty feet of soil. Some years ago the discovery was made that the earth from a mound in the Delta—that is to say, from the site of an ancient city—forms an excellent " top dressing" to spread over the fields : and the knowledge of this fact spread all over the fertile districts, and led to the digging away of all the mounds they contain. Within, all these mounds now present the appearance of a sponge or a dry honeycomb : for many of the walls and most of the street lines have been left as useless, while the mud that surrounded them has been carried away. At the proper season for the work, in the spring months, hundreds of men fill the mounds, and trains of donkeys and camels bear to the fields the earth that is dug out. Naturally in the course of the digging the men find antiquities also. But these are, upon an unwatched site, liable to destruction. Some are rescued by Arab dealers, who are well aware of the process and its results ; but of course they pay no attention to fragments ; and when any object has come into their hands, the place and circumstances of its discovery are almost always lost. But on this last point one must not speak too strongly, since it was from information supplied by one of these Arab dealers that the site of Naukratis was discovered. However, with them we are not now concerned ; for Mr. Petrie's vigorous measures against them in the previous season deterred any of them from making their appearance last year. When a site where the earth is being dug out is constantly watched, a most effectual and inexpensive manner of excavation offers itself. All objects, however insignificant, are sure to be brought and offered for sale : and by judicious management it is possible to secure all that are worth having. In this way many interesting things were obtained; but, above all, in this way the sites of the temples

of both Aphrodite and Hera were discovered. When any such site was found, it was of course necessary to avail oneself of the authority supplied by the official authorization of our work, and to stop all other digging upon the temple so discovered; but by taking the original finder himself on to the work, it was easy to avoid the danger of his being induced by the hope of further discoveries to conceal the place where he had found what he brought. To watch these independent workers, and to collect what they find, is a most necessary part of the excavator's duty; and an account of the season's work would be incomplete if it omitted to mention so important a help to acquisition and discovery.

(17) If I here add a few words about the system on which the work was conducted, it must be borne in mind that the system is Mr. Petrie's, and that I obtained it from him and preserved it in every essential particular. For his successful experience had already proved it to be practically advantageous; and the overseers and many of the workmen were already trained by him to follow it. If we set on one side all independent work on the part of the natives which had only to be watched for the sake of observing or acquiring any results it might produce, all our excavations may be divided into two classes. These may be roughly defined as piece-work and time-work. The system of piece-work was necessarily adopted wherever the constant presence of the overseers was impossible. A certain space for a pit or a trench was measured out, and a certain depth ordered : when the hole was completed its contents in cubic metres was measured, and payment was made accordingly : thus any man's slowness or laziness affected no one but himself, since the time he spent made no difference in the payment he received. But since this system, however convenient in many ways, encouraged rapid and careless digging, it obviously could not be adopted in any place where there

was a probability of the discovery of delicate or fragile objects, or of walls which must be cleared and left in their original position. In such cases therefore—in any case, indeed, where a site had been identified and was being thoroughly excavated—the second system had to be followed, and all the workpeople had to be paid by the day. This of course necessitated a daily register of their attendance. In receiving from workmen the antiquities they found in their work, we always allowed them just the same amount as we should have given for the same object to any one who had offered it for sale—a price better than any Arab dealer would be likely to give if he came that way. Thus there was no inducement·for them either to conceal anything found in the hope of selling it at a better price in another quarter, or to give a false account of the spot where any object had been discovered, whether the discovery was made within our work or outside it. For if falsehood offers no material advantage over truth, and at the same time involves the risk of detection and punishment, it is hardly likely to be preferred for its own sake, except by incorrigible offenders.

(18) It may be worth while to give a sketch of the way in which the day was generally spent at Naukratis, especially as such a sketch may serve to illustrate the manner in which work has been carried on there. Here again I shall be describing a plan which is, in all essential points, derived from Mr. Petrie's example : but I would refer rather to the later part of the time during which I was alone at Naukratis, when I had found out by experience the most convenient disposition and organization of my work.

By half-an-hour after sunrise all those employed by the day were expected to be in their places. Soon after this time I went round to the sites where they were working, varying from day to day the order of my visits. On each site I entered the names of all who were present for the day's work, and enrolled, if necessary, new workmen or filled the places of absentees. After seeing all the excavations well started, and giving directions for their continuation, I usually returned to the house at about nine or ten o'clock. Each time when I returned during the day, I had to unload myself of an accumulation of small antiquities, mostly bought up from those not actually in my employ : and to pay for these I filled my pockets, each time I went out, with a truly Spartan weight of money ; this weight may be realized by considering the fact that 5l. worth of the copper coinage of the country, which was sent down to me from Cairo for the sake of making these small purchases, weighed about 190 lbs. Hence it was obviously desirable to revisit the house several times in the day, both to leave my acquisitions and to obtain fresh supplies of copper. After breakfast, I went out again to look after my men till noon ; then I gave, from some central point, the signal for the hour of mid-day rest and food : as the days grew longer and the heat greater, this interval was naturally a little lengthened also. When it was past I again gave the signal for the renewal of work : and the uninterrupted time that remained before sunset afforded the best opportunity for carrying out any piece of excavation that required continuous personal care or supervision. In other cases, after I had seen the afternoon work started, I generally spent the next hour or two in visiting the parts of the mound where no excavation of my own was going on, in measuring the trenches finished by men who were digging by the metre, and in laying out new ones for them to go on with. As the hour of sunset approached, it became necessary to visit my workpeople again, and to sort, select, and roughly record all that they had found during the day. The value of anything which I kept was then entered to the account of its finder. On a site

like the cemetery, where separate graves were constantly being discovered, it was best to take at once the contents of each grave as they were found : these could then be laid aside and brought in together at sunset ; in the same way all the larger or heavier articles obtained from men who were not in my employ were labelled, if necessary, or enclosed in a wrappage, and left in charge of one of my overseers till evening. But on a site like the temenos of Aphrodite, where fragments, for the most part insignificant in themselves, were continuously being discovered, the only practicable way to deal with them was to allow all to accumulate till the end of the day : then, in the last few minutes, I had to inspect and to register whatever each had to offer as the result of his day's work ; though here too I could of course at any hour take over and lay aside any article of peculiar interest or fragility. When I saw the sun touch the horizon, I again gave the signal, and all returned home. Towards the end of my stay a usage sprang up which formed a most interesting and characteristic feature in our daily programme. Whatever may have been the interest or appreciation felt by my workpeople for the objects they were instrumental in discovering, they at least appreciated the material benefit which they themselves reaped from the large quantities in which these were found. Accordingly their rejoicing at the good fortune we had met with was unfeigned, and it spontaneously found for itself a means of expression. When the signal of sunset had been given, the people, instead of hurrying away to their homes, formed themselves every night into a kind of festal procession ; they had what the Arabs called a "fantasiyeh," this one was regularly known as the "fantasiyeh of the potsherds." Its order was usually after this fashion. The principal part of it started from the temple of Aphrodite. Several of the girls, selected by the overseer, raised upon their heads the baskets containing the potsherds and other small antiquities found during the day, and led off the procession; at their head went a piper, who came to meet them from the village, helped sometimes by one or two amateurs among the company. Then followed, in solemn state, my chief overseer, a splendid-looking Arab, and the rest of the workpeople in due order. At some point upon their homeward route they were joined by my other overseer and the people from his work, who fell into their places and swelled the procession, which, thanks to the flowing Arab dress, really had an impressive effect. I did not usually wait to accompany it, but went on in front to my house; there I distributed the contents of the various baskets among the heaps to which they belonged. In the evening not much was to be done beyond a rough sorting of what had been brought in, and recording as far as was possible at the time the results of the day.

Five days in every week were thus spent; and it is worthy of notice that during the whole of the four months, from December to March, there was not a single day on which work had to be suspended or even modified on account of the weather. All this time the shade temperature was moderate, usually keeping between 60° and 75° (Fahrenheit) in the daytime, though occasionally in March the thermometer went above 80°; at night it was cool, the extreme registered generally being between 40° and 50°. Thus it will be seen that the climate of the Delta in the winter will not seem at all unusual to one accustomed to that of England — except, indeed, for the duration and the intensity of the sunshine.

(19) When the season's work was drawing to a close, it became necessary to consider the packing of the antiquities that had been found, their exportation from Egypt, and their transport to England. In this matter, as indeed in every other, it is a pleasure to me to be able to acknowledge the considerate help and co-opera-

tion of Dr. R. S. Poole, then Secretary to the Egypt Exploration Fund. He not only at once responded to any request on my part, but often foresaw and provided against difficulties or delays that were likely to arise. Before our work began, we had come to an understanding with the authorities that we should be allowed to export most of the antiquities we discovered, on the condition that a certain portion of them should be selected to be kept at the Bulak Museum. At the end of the season, I made application to M. Maspéro, in order that this condition might be fulfilled; and I have to acknowledge the great courtesy with which he allowed me to bring only a few representative specimens to Bulak, and his care to select nothing for his museum which by its separation from the rest might injure the scientific completeness of any series of objects discovered at Naukratis. Meanwhile I had packed all the antiquities found during the season into about eighty cases; a somewhat deceptive bulk, owing, as has already been explained, to the impossibility of selecting at once the fragments of pottery that were worth keeping. Now I had only to bring these to Alexandria, whence the committee of the Fund had already provided for their transport by an Indian troop-ship. But there is one more acknowledgment that I must make before leaving this part of my account. From Mr. Cookson, H.B.M. Consul at Alexandria, I met with the greatest kindness and assistance in passing my boxes through the formalities that were still necessary before they could be shipped; an assistance which was most efficiently and willingly rendered to me by Mr. Harris, the chief constable of the Consulate, in whose care I ultimately left the boxes to await their despatch.

(20) Here ends the account of the discovery of the last season's antiquities at Naukratis, and of their exportation from Egypt. Before proceeding to a more detailed account of the

antiquities themselves, and of the various sites upon which they were found, it remains for me to say a few words about their condition and treatment after their safe arrival in England. I had all the more important cases brought to Cambridge, in order to work at them with plenty of room at my disposal: for this room I have to thank, first, the authorities of Gonville and Caius College, and later the director of the Fitzwilliam Museum. Most of my work at Cambridge calls for no notice beyond the publication of its results; but of the pottery from the temenos of Aphrodite a little may here be said. By gradual sorting and comparing, I have recovered some vases in an almost complete state, and about one half of others: many are represented by considerable pieces; others only by insignificant or isolated fragments. The total number of vases that have contributed their fragments to this vast layer of pieces must have been very large: and they must have been broken up before their fragments were cast out; for parts of the same vase were often found scattered to the east, the south, and the north of the temple. Indeed, in consequence of this confusion, I found it useless to preserve in sorting the distinctions of place that had been so far kept. As regards the condition of the vases, and the number of pieces into which they had been broken, the following figures will speak: of one large bowl, now nearly complete, about 70 fragments were found; of others again, that have been recovered only in part, I have counted the pieces of half-a-dozen of the first that came; these amounted to 47, 46, 77, 60, 31, and 17 respectively. As these were, as I have said, completely mixed up together with the remains of other similar vases, it will be clear that the task of separating them was one which required a considerable amount of time.

(21) The work of sorting and of mending has now been almost completed. In the British Museum will be found a representative selection of the various objects that have been recovered; the rest have been distributed among various museums, where it is hoped they may be seen and studied. For a specimen of the style of the pottery I would refer those who cannot see the vases themselves to the excellent coloured Plate in the Journal of Hellenic Studies, Pl. lxxxix (1887), as well as to the direct photographic reproductions in this volume.

(22) ONE of the most important sites to be looked for by the excavator of an early Greek city must always be the cemetery. For it was ever the custom to bury together with the dead various objects intended for their use or delectation. Such at least must originally have been the intention of this custom, even if in historical times its practice had survived the primitive beliefs out of which it arose. Hence it follows that from the imaginary needs of the dead we may learn much as to the real needs of the living; and the articles of use or of ornament that were adapted to fulfil those needs will be in both cases alike. The cemetery, then, must always be sought : but the clues that may lead to its discovery are not in all cases the same. In the case of most Greek sites two indications, perhaps, must be followed most carefully. Sometimes a rocky formation naturally lends itself to the excavation of caves and grottoes to receive the dead ; in this case the nature of the ground will often guide the explorer to his goal. Sometimes considerations of convenience are outweighed by the desire that the tombs may be conspicuous, and may record the burial of the deceased for the observation of all that pass by; if so, obviously the most fitting position will be beside the most frequented roads that lead to the city. Often, again, both objects will be combined, if a convenient face of rock is found beside a road. At first glance it might seem that considerations such as these could hardly lead to the discovery of the cemetery of Naukratis. The level surface of the delta is broken only by the low mounds that testify to the long-continued settlement of towns or villages, whose accumulating *débris* has gradually risen above the even plain. The ancient roads cannot be traced, nor if they could, would they lend us much help : for tombs could hardly be built beside them in the fields yearly overflowed by the Nile. Yet some mound, natural or artificial, must have been found wherein to bury the dead ; and perhaps it is easier to find the ancient thoroughfare near which the people of Naukratis placed their tombs than one might at first be disposed to imagine. Their traffic with the interior of the country may have been partly by land : but their communications with their own people, with those whose sympathy or remembrance were to be excited by conspicuous monuments, must have been exclusively by water. The canal therefore was the high-road beside which the graves of Naukratis were to be sought. Now as some low mounds lie to the north of the city, that is, in the direction of Greece, and near to the present bed of the canal, nearer still to what was probably its ancient course, these mounds seemed to be indicated by all circumstances as a likely site for the Greek cemetery.

(23) These anticipations, as has already been stated, were soon proved to be correct. The small mound to the north of the Arab village proved to be full of graves of Hellenic or Hellenistic period : but of monuments above the surface of the ground very little was discovered : if, as is most probable, they were of stone, there was little chance of their being

loft undisturbed. They seem not to have escaped this fate even in ancient times; for the only two sculptured stelae of the ordinary type that come from Naukratis were found within the limits of the ancient city. As burials cannot have been allowed to take place within these limits, it must follow that they were in ancient times converted from monumental to practical use; one of them with its face downward formed part of a later pavement. To these must be added the curious stele found in the previous year in or near[1] the temenos of the Dioscuri, bearing the inscription Τεάω εἰμὶ σῆμα,[2] "I am the gravestone of Teaos." The two sculptured stelae found last year have no inscription upon them. The first is in very low relief, of an execution too good for any period but the fourth century; in its subject and treatment it resembles the well-known Attic grave-stones of the time. Though a portion of it is gone, one figure, that of a boy, is still complete, and is very graceful in pose and character; two other figures can also be distinguished. The whole seems once to have represented one of those scenes of greeting or departure that are so common upon gravestones of the finest period.

The other stele, though far inferior in execution, is interesting from its subject. It is a good and very complete representation of the scene so often recurring upon Greek sepulchral reliefs, the scene known commonly as the funeral banquet. Here we see a man with a somewhat cumbrous garland around his head, reclining upon a couch and supported on his left elbow: his breast is bare, and a mantle is wrapped round his legs; his left hand holds a cup, his right rests on the edge of the couch, just above the table that is before it. By his feet sits his wife, her feet resting on a foot-

stool: in her left hand she holds a shallow cup, out of which drinks a serpent, which coils round over her left shoulder: her head has been carefully chiselled away. Two boys wait on the pair; the one on the left is clothed in a mantle which he supports with his left arm; his right hand is raised as if to beckon. The other boy holds a jug (œnochoe) in his left hand; with his right he offers a cup to his master. The dress of this boy is very peculiar; it seems to consist of a single close-fitting garment of some smooth hard material, terminating on the arms and legs in short sleeves and drawers. An ample feast is provided; on the table are cakes and fruit, as well as a cup: on a low stand by the head of the couch is a large bowl, doubtless for mixing the wine; on its rim and on a stand behind are several smaller vases. All the furniture is also sumptuous; the couch has elaborately-turned legs, and is provided with tasselled hangings; the table and footstool are of ornamental construction, their legs terminating in lions' feet: even the large mixing bowl has a design upon it. Above this scene, in the corner to the left, is a square window, through which is seen a horse's head, ready bridled, as if to take its master upon a journey. The whole is set in an architectural frame; on each side is an Ionic column : on them rests a narrow entablature, its frieze divided as if into small metopes; above is a pediment with curved top, and a round disc like a shield in its centre; a tone end remains an acroterion of palmetto design. The subject of this relief need not long detain us: it is of a well-known type, which has often been discussed; I need only refer to Prof. Percy Gardner's paper in the Journal of Hellenic Studies for 1885, where other authorities are quoted. It seems that the feast typifies the enjoyment by the dead of the offerings made by survivors at his tomb; with this thought is mingled one of his life in another world. Two somewhat inconsistent symbols are here, as often, introduced;

---

[1] It is hard to define the exact boundary of the temenos in the region where this stele was found.

[2] Nauk. I., Pl. XXX. 15; p. 62.

the serpent, in whose form the departed is often looked upon as accepting the food offered to him; and the horse, the symbol of departure to a far country.

The style of the relief calls for more attention. So far as the art is Greek, it is of small interest, for it is obviously of a late and degenerate period : but many characteristics of the treatment are not Greek. These are most apparent in the small attendant on the left of the scene. The peculiar treatment of the head, especially of the eye, which is represented in full though the face is in profile, the awkward and stiff position of the arms, the backward curve of the fingers, all are mannerisms copied from Egyptian models. The same peculiarities recur elsewhere, for instance in the right hand of the reclining man, and the right arm and hand of the attendant on the right, whose dress also is not Greek. The relief must date from Ptolemaic or possibly Roman times; and here we see the degenerate and failing art of Greece taking to itself just those mannerisms and defects of an alien style which it would soonest have rejected in its earlier and better days. The archaic Greek artists may have learnt something from Egypt : but what they sought was help in the difficulty of material expression, not meaningless and lifeless conventionalities.

I have said that no sepulchral reliefs were found during the excavations in the cemetery itself; but one monument of a similar character appeared. This was a small slab of stone, of about the same size and form as the relief just described ; but it was surrounded only by a plain raised border, and surmounted by a triangular pediment. The plain surface thus left within a sort of frame had evidently once been decorated by painting : but though I thought, upon a long and careful examination of the stone, I could detect some traces of the design that it once bore, those traces were not clear enough to indicate either the colours used or the subject represented. Another stone monument, of a

much more complicated character, was discovered in the cemetery. The fragments that came to light were some portions of Ionic or Corinthian columns, probably once decorating the face of a heroum : they clearly adorned the front of a wall as they are fluted only on one side. One drum was $9\frac{1}{2}$ inches high, and $8\frac{1}{4}$ in diameter ; a base was $5\frac{1}{4}$ inches in height, its diameter at the bottom was 14 inches, at the top 11. From these measurements it is possible to gain some notion of the dimensions of the monument to which the columns belonged: it is the only tomb of any architectural pretensions of which any trace has been found at Naukratis.

(24) So far we have been considering only such grave-buildings as were originally above the surface of the ground ; many such must probably have once existed, though they have now disappeared. But structures beneath the earth would probably still remain, if they had ever been made; hence it is more significant in their case to observe how little of them came to light. No built tomb-chambers or even graves were found, except one or two graves of burnt brick, dating from Roman times. In one case some remains of fresco painting, of a blue colour, were found ; this colour seems to have been applied directly to the mud-brick wall, now indistinguishable from the mud that surrounds it ; in another instance a grave was lined with a thin coating of stucco. But these were exceptional instances ; as a rule there was no sign that any elaborate preparations had been made for the burial, except making a new pit to receive the coffin. For the body seems always to have been buried in a coffin of some sort; I saw no traces of the practice of cremation.[3] Nor, on the other hand, do the Greeks of Naukratis seem to have been influenced at all by the Egyptian custom of embalming their dead. The body had

---

[3] Except, perhaps, in one instance ; see below, p. 27.

always completely disappeared; even the bones could not often be distinguished, and in no case were they well enough preserved to admit of their being kept. It was not uncommon, especially in the case of the richer graves, to place a layer of white sand beneath the body or coffin; a proceeding most convenient for the excavator, as such a layer can easily be distinguished in the black mud; and thus it is made possible to clear a grave carefully by itself. In one case, also, I found a thin pavement of plaster beneath a coffin of terra-cotta; but this coffin was exceptional in shape; thus it, as well as the bed on which it is laid, seems not to have been in accordance with the ordinary customs of Naukratis.

(25) The coffins themselves call for more particular notice; they may be classified according to the material of which they were made, stone, terra-cotta, or wood. Only one of stone was found in its original position in the cemetery; this was a rough sarcophagus, devoid of all ornamentation. It was of massive proportions and only roughly finished. The body of the sarcophagus was 8 feet in length, 3 feet 8 inches in breadth at the top, 2 feet 9 inches in depth, externally: its sides and bottom were 8 inches thick. The lid was a flat slab, 18 inches high, with its edges bevelled on the upper side. Within this sarcophagus was nothing but a few small bronze nails, that seemed to come from a decayed wooden coffin, and the bones of the occupant, now barely distinguishable. I saw one or two other plain sarcophagi in the neighbourhood of Naukratis, which had probably been found under the Arab village on the north mound; I do not think the small mound I cleared had been disturbed before.

The two other materials are far commoner. The coffins of terra-cotta, of about the same consistency as an ordinary tile, were in every case crushed in by the pressure of the earth; but it was easy enough to see what their shape

and construction must have been. They were usually made in two pieces, one to contain the head, the other the feet of the corpse; and one of the ends usually, but not always, had a projecting flange at the junction. Each half was usually about 35 or 36 inches in length, 20 to 12 in breadth, and about 16 to 9 in depth, the last two dimensions being largest in the middle of the coffin and diminishing towards its ends. The coffin was quite plain, and had no ornamentation of any sort. But one or two exceptions to this rule called for notice. I have already mentioned the coffin of peculiar shape that lay upon a thin bed of plaster. This coffin was shaped at the top to fit the head and shoulders of the corpse, so as to present a trefoil outline; from the shoulders to the feet it narrowed in even lines. I found in one case a hand in rough terra-cotta, the size and shape of a child's; this seemed to belong to an anthropoid coffin, with a representation on the lid of the form of the deceased; but no other traces of such coffins were found. I may also mention here two beasts' paws of terra-cotta, though their connection with a coffin or anything else likely to have been buried in this cemetery cannot well be traced.

While we are speaking of earthenware coffins, another similar method of interment may be mentioned: it seems to have been used mostly in the case of young children, as is indicated by the bones discovered. A coffin was not made, but an amphora was used for the purpose; its top was broken off to allow the body to be inserted; in one case I found the top lying across the neck, in undisturbed earth, so that it must have been buried so. To judge from the shape and fabric of the amphorae, this practice must have been common at all times, from the sixth or fifth century down to the Ptolemaic or even the Roman Period. In one case were found the handles of an amphora of the shape reproduced in Naukratis I., Pl. xvii. 17; later forms were more common.

(26) From the third material that was used for coffins, wood, one might at first thought expect the least remains. This expectation is indeed fulfilled as far as the coffins themselves are concerned; the wood has completely disappeared in every case. But the beautiful terra-cotta ornaments with which they were once decorated have been found in great numbers: these were gorgoneia, of which about eighty-five were found in almost perfect preservation, gryphons, and rosettes of various sizes and designs. The coffins themselves were probably of the same shape as one in the Bulak Museum, pointed out to me by M. Maspéro: it is of Greek workmanship, but comes from a drier soil; and consequently the wood of which it is made has remained. This coffin consists of an oblong box, and a gable-shaped lid, which presents a high-pitched pediment at each end. These pediments, as well as the rest of the coffin, are divided into panels, and ornamented with painting and with terra-cotta reliefs, which are not, however, of so fine work as those found at Naukratis: there are small gorgoneia affixed to the extremities of the round beams that run from end to end of the coffin, along its angles. A similar arrangement would account for the numerous small terra-cotta ornaments that were found in the cemetery of Naukratis wherever a wooden coffin had once been buried. Some specimens of these ornaments have been reproduced upon Plate XVI. 1—6. I have called the small terra-cotta masks gorgoneia; it will be observed that some of these have a pair of small wings springing from the forehead. Mr. Cecil Smith has suggested to me that they should rather be regarded as heads of Hypnos; when we remember the close relationship between Sleep and Death, such figures seem particularly appropriate upon a coffin; and the winged type in particular approaches very closely to that sometimes assumed by the god of sleep. But in spite of these arguments, I am still inclined to retain

the name gorgoneia.[1] The coffins were of essentially architectural construction; and these ornaments seem to correspond to the terra-cotta antefixes which we usually find in real buildings. A very common form taken by these antefixes is that of the gorgon's head, originally of the grinning and hideous type that is in early times proper to the monster: thus they resemble in character, and perhaps in intention, the monstrous gargoyles of the mediæval cathedral. But the gorgon type, as is well known, lost in later times all its hideous or terrible character; and it is to the type best known in the "Medusa Rondanini" at Munich that our examples most nearly conform. In the suppression of characteristic attributes, they have gone yet farther; for none of them preserve even the conventional knot of snakes beneath the chin; the bow above the forehead may be a reminiscence of this, but it is a mere blue riband as here represented.

The terra-cotta masks have in many cases preserved traces of colour: the face is white, the hair red, and the riband that ties it blue; sometimes the eyes also are coloured, the iris being red, the outlines darker: gilding is also used for ornamental parts in some instances. Beside the masks of terra-cotta, which were all of the same type, though varying in their size and execution, I also found two or three of white plaster, of a slightly different shape (Pl. XVI. 5). These also had traces of colour, especially in the eyes.

It is possible to fix with some precision the date of the coffins on which the gorgoneia were used. From the style, which, though already tending to more prettiness, generally shows good and careful work, they would seem to belong to the end of the fourth century, or the earlier years of the Ptolemaic period. Fortunately, however, we have other evidence by which to test this view: with one of the masks

[1] In this view I am confirmed by M. J. Six, whose treatise, de Gorgone, is the standard work on the subject.

was found a bronze coin, having on the obverse the head of Alexander with the elephant's skin, on the reverse the eagle—the well-known Ptolemaic types. This coin seemed from its style to belong to one of the earliest members of the dynasty; thus it fully confirms the date that we were led by other considerations to assign to these gorgoneia.

Other ornaments, such as gryphons, bucrania, and rosettes of various types and sizes, need not long detain us; specimens of these are given on Plate XVI. 8—14. They also were enriched by gilding and painting, and probably once served to ornament coffins of a similar period.

(27) We must now turn to the contents of the graves, the objects of use or ornament that were buried with the dead. Here we meet with greater variety both in the date of the burials and in the nature of the objects recovered: but unfortunately graves from the sixth century, the time when Naukratis was in its greatest prosperity, are still almost entirely lacking. Here perhaps the disappointment is greater than in any other case; for we might have hoped for some complete or even unbroken specimens of the magnificent vases that we know to have been made at Naukratis. This hope has in no way been fulfilled, whether because these vases were for the temple and not for the tomb, or because the cemetery of the sixth century has not been found. Early graves are, indeed, very rare; the richest ones all date from the fourth or third century B.C. I have been able to make a catalogue of the contents of about seventy-five different graves; but it does not seem worth while to reproduce it entirely here; a few selections will give an adequate notion of its nature. To explain my notation I must state that I called the five trenches, running north and south, A B C D E, beginning from the east; and also divided the mound by cross lines into sections which I

numbered 1—5, from south to north. But I was not able to draw much distinction between the graves found in different parts of the mound. With this explanation, a few extracts from my catalogue will be intelligible.

Grave C 2, 3 metres deep.
1. Rough red terra-cotta head of animal.
2. Bronze bangle.
3. Iron bangle.
4. Iron comb.
5. Alabastron.

Grave C 3, 3½ metres deep.
1. Black vase, ornamented with projecting dots.
2. Iron and bronze strigil.

Grave C 3, 3½ metres deep.
1. Bronze mirror.
2. Minute gorgoneion.
3. Lecythus, with diamond pattern of black lines, and white spots, on red ground.
4. Minute black jug, with small neck.

Grave C 4, 3 metres deep.
1. Bottom of bowl.
2. Cowries.
3. Bone beads.
4. Shells.
5. Piece of lead.
6. Claw of lobster.

Grave C 4, 3 metres deep.
1. Alabastron.
2. Lecythi, plain.
3. Lecythus, diamond pattern, with white spots.
4. Black lamp.
5. Lecythus with head, and white touches added.
6. Black and red bowl.

Grave D 1, 1 metre deep.
1.⎱Vases tapering towards both ends, rough
2.⎰ red ware.
3.⎱Alabastra.
4.⎰
5. Black vase, with white lines.
6. Smoothed tridacna shell.

7. Shell.
8. Gryphons.
9. Bucrania. ⎫
10. Terra-cotta horns. ⎬ from coffin.
11. Gorgoneia. ⎭

Grave D 2, 2 metres deep.

1. Large alabastron.
2. Lecythus, ornamented with projecting dots below, and painted with figures in white blue and gold, with relief (Pl. XVI. 20).

Examples like these might be indefinitely multiplied; but enough have already been given to show the usual contents of a grave. They are disappointing, indeed, when compared with the expectations we might have had; yet perhaps they are not without some value, as dating from a period of which very few remains were found in the town, and tending to show that it is not by a mere accident that almost all the things found at Naukratis date from an earlier time. For those who could not afford to bury more than this with their dead, are hardly likely to have left behind them in their life many objects that would repay the search of the excavator.

(28) It only remains for us to notice briefly any of the things found in the excavation of the cemetery that seem worthy of individual attention; these we may classify under various heads:—1. Vases; 2. Articles for personal use or adornment; 3. Other furniture of the tomb.

1. Vases. It has already been stated that the cemetery yielded little or nothing to enlighten us as to the great Naukratite manufacture of vases in the sixth century. Hardly any individual fragments of pottery have been found which can with certainty be assigned to so early a date; much less any perfect specimens of the vases of that period. One or two small vases were found which seem to go back at least into the fifth century; but even these were exceptions, most of the graves are not

much earlier than the beginning of the Ptolemies. Among the vases or fragments which seem distinctly early were a small vase with red lines on a yellow ground; some Cyrenaic fragments; two large rough plates of yellow ware, of the same description as those found last year in the lower strata of the trench in the temenos of Apollo; and a vase of very peculiar shape, like an askion with a vertical hole through the middle (Pl. XVI. 19). A small urn with four handles and red ornamentation on a yellow ground also seems to be of early style; it was found together with the contents of a later grave, but this was probably a mere accident. The urn seemed to contain ashes; if so, it yields the only trace I found of the practice of cremation—a fact of some interest in one of the earliest interments. But the facts are not certain enough to be insisted upon. The urn was broken when discovered, and its contents may not have been human remains.

Vases of the ordinary red ware, either completely covered with black varnish, or with circles of the red ground visible, were common enough—among them some drinking cups of graceful shapes, canthari and cylices. A not unusual shape was that of a plain bowl, with two horizontal handles just beneath the rim. Three of these are of interest, two from inscriptions incised on their bottoms, one for the figures upon its sides. The first of these bears the graffito ΛΔΓΙ on one part of the bottom, opposite it ΔΙΙΙΙ, the other has ⊣ΔΔΔΔ, and in the middle of the bottom, ΔΔΓ : here it is obvious that we have numbers, and ⊣ seems the sign for drachmas, ⊢, retrograde; thus we may read the first 16 drachmas, 14; the second 40 drachmas, 25.[5] The meaning of the figures cannot be so easily be conjectured. Plain bowls like this could hardly have cost more than a drachma a piece, so that the number can hardly refer to

---

[5] An Attic writer, wishing to express 16 drachmas, would have written ΔΓ⊢.

the lot of vases for which the sum was paid—unless, indeed, that lot contained some larger or more elaborate vases. Mr. Petrie made the ingenious suggestion that we may here have a record of the undertaker's bill. Graffiti of this kind are not very common, and it is hardly possible to determine their meaning in all cases; often, perhaps, it was not meant to be understood by any but the writer. The third of these bowls is ornamented with two scenes, in the ordinary red-figured style of the fourth century : under each handle is a palmetto design; on one side is a seated Satyr, holding a thyrsus ; before him stands a draped female, holding a cup; on the other side is a hunter standing, with one foot supported on a rock; he holds two spears; in front of him is another male figure, now much damaged, but seemingly of comic or grotesque character; the two suggest a resemblance to two figures on the Ficoroni cista, derived perhaps from the same source.

Small lecythi were of course abundant; these were either plain, or ornamented with a palmetto or other design : this was often a male or female head, in one case a crouching hare. Another common ornamentation was a diamond pattern of black lines crossing, with dots of white on the intersections. One lecythus (Pl. XVI. 20) calls for especial mention; it is the one already referred to in the catalogue of various graves. Unfortunately the mouth and handle are lost, but the rest is perfect : its body tapers towards the top, and its lower part, which is thicker, is studded with projecting dots, so as to give the whole a resemblance in appearance to an elongated acorn ; on the smooth part is a rich design; beneath the handle is an elaborate palmetto, but in front is a scene painted with all the richness of polychromy. In the middle is Eros,[6] white, with gold and blue wings, mount-

ing a ladder, and holding a small censer in his hand ; on each side of him is a female figure, one seated, one standing ; their skin is white, their drapery blue and red, and gold ornaments are added here and there in relief.

Various plain or rough vases were also found, some tapering from the middle towards both ends ; also some miniature amphoræ, one carefully worked to imitate an almond in shape and appearance (Pl. XVI. 15).

2. Articles for personal use or adornment. Here must be mentioned various articles of toilet; several bronze mirrors were found, and one mirror case, but all were either quite plain or had only the simplest ornamentation; some combs came to light, both of iron and bronze, and two or three toilet pots, one of lead (?), two of pottery ; one of these still contained its rouge, quite fresh and ready for use ; on its lid was painted a tripod; strigils both of bronze and of iron were also pretty common ; there were also some long and narrow bars of bronze, terminating in a minute spoon-bowl, apparently medical implements (Pl. XVI. 17). Among personal ornaments the commonest were bangles, both of iron and bronze, usually of very small size, and some rings ; most of the latter were either plain, or too much damaged to retain any design ; but there was one exception. This was a bronze ring plated with gold ; on it was a beautifully executed intaglio, representing Eros crouching, and apparently holding a wreath on a stick—doubtless a scene from some popular game (Pl. XVII. 7). Some remains of silver ornaments were also found, but in very bad condition ; beads were very rare ; here perhaps we may also mention some small bronze bells, with iron clappers (Pl. XVI. 7); several of these were found, but it is not clear whether they were attached to the dress, or buried with the deceased for other purposes.

---

[6] This scene seems to represent the gathering of the incense, according to a suggestion of Dr. Furtwängler quoted in M. Froehner's catalogue of the Exhibition of the Bur-

lington Fine Arts Club, 1888, p. 18. There two or three other instances of the same scene are quoted.

3. Other furniture of the tomb. Alabastra were often found, both of alabaster, often so corroded by damp as to be mere skeletons, and of other materials made in imitation, whether terra-cotta or faience. In one grave were found two massive and shallow bowls of alabaster, narrowing at the top; two or three lecythi of alabaster came to light. A leaden bottle too was discovered, and several pieces of lead; also several large shells which must have been used for some practical purpose, probably to hold food or other necessaries. Two or three of these were plain tridacna shells. Here may be mentioned some curious minute saucers, sometimes with two handles, and lamps of various periods and shapes, including most of the prevalent Greek types. In one case an iron spear-head was found, but this was exceptional. Two or three graves yielded small amulets in bone or faience, representing the god Bes.

Many large iron and bronze nails had doubtless once served to hold together the wooden coffins. In only two or three cases terra-cotta statuettes were found. The two best examples are reproduced upon Pl. XVI. 16, 18. One is a single figure of a boy; the other a group of Eros and Psyche, worked as in relief, and hollow at the back. On this some traces of gilding and colour remained.

(29) But it would be tedious to carry this enumeration into further details. Enough has been said to indicate the nature of the objects discovered, and to show that they date mostly from a time when Naukratis was already declining. But though we may not have gained from the cemetery, or this part of it, the results that might have been hoped for, it may perhaps have yielded some results that are not without their interest.

CHAPTER III.

TEMPLE OF THE DIOSCURI.

(30) THE discovery of the temple of the Dioscuri has already been mentioned in the first chapter. Its remaining walls and pillars, as well as its probable plan, are indicated upon Pl. I. The hatched parts represent the brickwork that was still extant, the outlines give what is an all but certain restoration.

Walls and pillars alike were built of unbaked mud-brick—a dark structure, hardly now to be distinguished from the dark mud that surrounds it, but for the divisions often visible between the bricks and courses. This brickwork must always have been unsightly, and so we find it to have been covered by a coat of plaster. On the pillars in front, this plaster was still in its place, and presented a plain white surface to the view: the stucco had, however, peeled off the inner walls of the cella of the temple, but was found in considerable quantities at their foot, lying upon the floor of the building. To this stucco we must again refer, because of the colour that remained upon it: but first it is necessary to say a few words as to the plan of the temple. A glance at the plate will show that it consisted of a single chamber, and was a variety, though a peculiar one, of the ordinary temple "in antis." Only a small portion of the cella walls remained; that on the north was almost perfect, being only broken by a gap formed in sinking a well at a later period. The east wall could not so easily be traced; the portion marked as extant upon the plan was extremely difficult to distinguish from the surrounding mud, and may possibly be inserted by a mistake. No trace of a door or of a second chamber behind was to be found, but this too is a fact that must not be too strongly insisted on, in consideration of the difficulty of distinguishing wall from mud in this region. The southern wall has entirely disappeared, and has been assumed to correspond exactly to the northern one. Of the pillars on the west three remain in part; and the extant portions exactly correspond in their size and position to the requirements of a symmetrical portico of four pillars. If the pillars themselves were 34[1] inches by 17, and the intercolumniations five times the breadth of the pillars, or 85 inches—measurements which are as nearly as possible those of the extant parts—we obtain a total width for the colonnade which is almost precisely that actually found by the most careful measurement.[2] Hence it follows that all the essential parts of the temple must have been as indicated in the plan; and though this plan is a very peculiar one, it does not admit of much doubt as to its characteristic features. The temple is, as has been already said, "in antis;" but the antæ, or ends of the cella walls, are not, as is usual, in a line with the front row of pillars, but project considerably beyond them. Again, these are oblong pillars, not round columns—a peculiarity due doubtless to the nature of the material that is used; then the arrangement also of the pillars is curious; the one at each end has its outer side contiguous to the cella wall. Thus the projecting antæ, doubtless covered by a gable roof, enclosed a sort of

---

[1] Or perhaps 28½ inches at first; in the only complete one, a layer of plaster was visible at this distance from the front.

[2] The measurements and levels of the temple were taken by Mr. Petrie before he left; I also verified them afterwards.

pronaos, separated by the row of pillars from the cella inside. It is worthy of notice also that the temple faces westward, as was usual in the case of buildings dedicated to demigods or heroes like the Dioscuri: while the temples of the gods usually opened towards the east.

(31) The fragments of stucco from the inner walls of the cella were of great interest, because they bore upon their surface, in wonderfully good preservation, the fresco painting that once adorned them. The colours used were very brilliant—red and blue on a white ground;[1] here and there, perhaps, a little yellow; but this may be due merely to the discolouring of the stucco. The designs consisted exclusively of decorative patterns; and though no fragment was found that was large enough to admit of a complete restoration of the patterns used, it was clear that most of the pieces came from a mæander design, varied apparently with stars within squares—a practice not uncommon in early Greek decorative work.

(32) Beyond the plan of the temple itself, the second season's excavations made but a small addition to the number of the objects found in the temenos of the Dioscuri. No more fragments of the fine dedicated bowl, found in the previous season, and reproduced in Naukratis I., Pl. VI. 6, were recovered. Nor were many other important pieces of pottery to be seen; one, however, is interesting; it represents men seated in a boat upon a sea of white waves, and above is a piece of a wing; it seems probable that the subject of the representation was the sirens singing to

Odysseus. The design is black on red; but the types of the faces are curious; the treatment of the waves with a wash of thick, white pigment in wavy lines, is most peculiar. So far as I know, this fragment is quite isolated in style, and it merits more attention than can here be bestowed upon it; it is to be seen at the British Museum. The style of this piece can hardly be later than the sixth century; other fragments of the same period came to light; but none of them call for especial notice. Several more inscriptions record dedications to the Dioscuri, thus proving, if more proof be needed, that the temple and temenos do belong to those deities. One other inscription, which was incised upon a piece of rough pottery, is of interest, as it contains a portion of a dedication to Apollo. It was evidently a piece of a broken vessel that had wandered a short distance from the neighbouring temenos of the Milesian Apollo; but as it was buried in undisturbed earth, at a depth of some eighteen inches below the bottom of the pillar that was nearest to it, it clearly must have been buried there before the temple of the Dioscuri was built.

(33) This fact leads us to the last question we need consider in connection with this temple—that of its age. There is very little definite evidence afforded by the objects discovered; many of them may not have belonged to the actual building which was found; the frescoes can hardly supply any indication of period. There is, however, no reason for supposing this temple to be of a very high antiquity. The fragment from the temenos of Apollo just referred to seems to indicate that the temple of the Dioscuri is later at least than the earliest one dedicated to Apollo. The plan and construction of the temple, again, though it is peculiar, is not necessarily of very early date. On the whole, there is not evidence enough to outweigh that afforded by the level of the foundation, which can be compared with

---

[1] I am indebted to Prof. Middleton for the following facts as to the pigments used, &c.: "The *blue* is made of powdered glass coloured with some salt of copper and then mixed with lime. The *red* is a pure oxide of iron. The *stucco* is the most wonderful stuff I ever saw—very much harder than English Portland stone. It is made of about 3 parts of lime to 1 of finely-ground silica or quartz—probably local sand; it has been made with extremest skill and care. None like it could be made now."

that of the Temple of Apollo and other neighbouring buildings; the ground on which they all were built was probably quite level originally. The bases of the pillars vary from 310 to 316½ inches above Mr. Petrie's datum, the north wall was 303 inches, but its foundation may have been a little deepened for support. It would thus appear that the temple of the Dioscuri, as we found it, was nearly contemporary with the second temple and temenos-wall of Apollo.[1] If this be true, it dates from about the middle of the fifth century B.C.; from the time, that is, when Naukratis began to revive from the calamity that seems to have befallen it near the end of the sixth century. The archaic pottery and the earlier dedications must in that case be regarded as survivals from an earlier temple that once occupied the same site. Thus, though the evidence here is scantier, we may suppose that the Dioscuri as well as other divinities at Naukratis had in their temenos successive temples, built in different periods of the city's growth and prosperity.

---

[1] Nauk. I., p. 16, Pl. IV.

CHAPTER IV.

(34) IN the first chapter an account has already been given of the way in which the site dedicated to Aphrodite at Naukratis was discovered; how it was first identified by the fortuitous discovery of inscriptions, how the walls of the Ptolemaic temple were then recognized, and how finally two earlier foundations were found beneath them, and the boundaries of the temenos itself could be traced. We must now reverse the order of our description, and endeavour to sketch briefly the architectural history of this ancient sanctuary, beginning from the lowest and earliest level. Fortunately the materials for such a sketch are in this case exceptionally complete; upon Plates I., II., III., they will be found in a convenient form for reference. Plate I., in its upper part, contains a general plan of the temple and temenos. In this plan the various levels of the foundations of the various walls are distinguished by different manners of hatching, and thus it is easy to see at a glance what parts of the building are of the same level, and, therefore, probably contemporary; walls reconstructed at various levels are indicated as belonging to the lowest level at which they occur. Plate II. is a plan on double the scale, showing in detail the various levels of construction that are found in the temple itself. Plate III., on the same scale as Plate II., gives the sections along the two lines drawn on Plates I. and II., from W. to E., and from S. to N. On this plate are indicated, beside the walls, the places where the stratum of pottery and other fragments was found. In it is also added, at the sides, a scale of levels: these are taken from the

arbitrary datum fixed, as a convenient one, by Mr. Petrie last year—a point 500 inches below a certain conspicuous platform of Roman brick on the east of the cleared part of the ancient town. Thus Plate III. may be compared with Plate XLVI. in Naukratis, Part I.; but in comparing the actual levels we must take into account certain considerations that will afterwards be noticed. After so much explanation of our plates, we may now proceed to the history of the temple itself.

(35) The earliest temple of Aphrodite and the great altar that stood in front of its eastern door were founded upon the hard mud that everywhere underlies the town of Naukratis. This mud is always reached by the excavator as soon as he has cleared away all the artificial accumulation that generations of occupants have heaped above it. Its surface is represented on the section by a thick black line. If its level, as here indicated, be compared with that of the original surface of the ground in the temenos of Apollo, Naukratis I., Pl. XLVI., a difference of about twenty inches will be observed; but this is hardly more than may be due to an accident, though the ground was probably almost perfectly level before the city was built; for the two sites are nearly a quarter of a mile apart. We have, then, every reason for believing that the temple of Aphrodite was one of the earliest religious foundations at Naukratis, or at least that it was the first building to occupy the site on which it stands; and that site is so central that it can hardly have been left bare in the prosperous days of

E

the city—certainly not when the Hellenion was founded, for it lies between that and the temenos of Apollo, in the most populous part of the town. We may, however, see reason hereafter to suppose that the southern part of the town, where the Hellenion lies, was of later date than the more northerly neighbourhood of the temple of Apollo; but in any case the scarab factory and its surroundings, which are close to the temple of Aphrodite, are anterior to the reign of Amasis, when the Hellenion was founded. But these chronological questions must be considered together in a later chapter. Here we need only note that the only literary reference to the Aphrodite of Naukratis and her temple, that of Athenæus, mentions as a date the 23rd Olympiad (688 B.C.), and though this seems impossibly early, the whole story that he tells clearly does belong to an early period in Greek history.

If we now turn to the extant remains themselves, we may notice first that there are no dug-out foundations. Such are rarely if ever found at Naukratis for structures of mud-brick such as this temple. And the test of time has fully justified a proceeding that might at first sight appear to show lack of care in the builder.

The earliest temple is a simple and regular oblong building, with a door in its eastern wall; within, it is divided into two compartments, the cella or naos proper and the opisthodomus, by a smaller wall, having a door for communication in the midst. The position of this doorway, as well as of that in the east wall of the temple, could only be traced by carefully following‘with a knife the edge of the plaster floor; the earth that had filled it could not be distinguished from the mud-brick wall on either side. The walls were covered within by a thin coat of plaster; on this no signs of decoration, either by painting or otherwise, could be seen : but the plaster itself remained over a considerable portion of the surface of the walls. A similar

but somewhat thicker coat of plaster formed the floor of the temple. At some period not very long after the first building it was found necessary to raise this floor; and accordingly a second horizontal layer of plaster is found at a level about a foot above the first. This later floor extends also over the part of the precinct in front of the temple, and between the temple and the great altar.

This altar consists of a thin case of mud-brick walls, filled inside with ashes, doubtless those of victims that had been burnt in sacrifice to the Goddess Aphrodite.

Thus it reminds us of the great altar of Zeus at Olympia, which was also constructed of the ashes of victims; it is cased outside with a double layer of plaster, dating from two different periods. In front of the altar is a flight of steps leading up from the temple, and on each side is a small wing; these are all of mud-brick faced with plaster; the altar itself is surmounted by a small cornice. But the altar and its appurtenances cannot be thus simply described. For we may observe various stages in its history and construction which, if not very interesting in themselves, are of importance as throwing some light on the history of the temple and its precinct. It is clear from the plan that the altar was completely buried before the second temple was built, but we may notice four stages in its previous history.

1. The altar itself and a flight of three steps leading up to it were built, resting on the basal mud; at the same level is also a foundation of the south wing : the whole was coated with plaster.

2. Fifteen inches higher (level 315); when the temple had a new floor given to it, that floor extended over the precinct in front also; and on it was founded a new flight of four steps leading up to the altar.

3. Seven inches higher still (level 322); when the lowest of the four new steps was buried in the accumulation, the south wing was

rebuilt, and a north wing also was added.[1] At the same time the altar was covered with a new coat of plaster above the old one.

4. On both wings later constructions of mud-brick were added, to raise the level of their tops.

These facts seem to show that the accumulation of the earth in the temenos round the altar took place gradually, and that it had to be altered from time to time in consequence. The walls of the temenos, as we shall see, point to a similar conclusion. The question is a difficult one, and can hardly be settled apart from a consideration of the various strata found in excavating the site.

The shape of the temenos is irregular, being probably determined by the boundaries of other properties or by roads. On the north, south and west, and also on the northern part of the east side, the wall that bounds it seems to have been built at the same time as the temple itself, and to have remained through the later periods; this may clearly be seen by a glance at the plan (Pl. I.), and sections (Pl. III.). Another part of the enclosure wall on the eastern side was built at a later time, but apparently before the foundation of the second temple. In the northern part of the enclosure were two wells, constructed of cylinders of pottery, ten inches in height; these wells descended to a depth of twenty feet and twenty-three feet respectively: there were also in each case holes in the cylinders, to facilitate descent. In the first well, which was thirty-five inches in diameter, there were four such holes in the top cylinder, two in the third and fifth, and so on. The second was thirty-three inches in diameter, and had two holes, about twenty inches apart, in each cylinder, but these were not arranged in

any vertical succession above one another. It was clear from the level of the wells that they both belonged to the first temple, and that in later times they were forgotten or lost, and buried in earth and refuse. Yet the second well as soon as it was cleared out yielded a plentiful supply of good water, which was used all the rest of the season both by my own workpeople and by others in the neighbourhood.

(36) The problem that next meets us is one of great difficulty. On the section are marked the places where "fragments of pottery, &c.," were found. They were mingled with statuettes and parts of statuettes, ashes and bones, all in the utmost confusion. This strange mixture lay almost entirely in two layers, one just above the level of the earliest floor; another just below the level of the floor of the second temple; between the two layers was a thick stratum of dark sand; the lower was much thicker and richer than the upper. Both layers extended over the whole surface of the temenos, on the north, south, and east of the temple; behind it, on the west, only a few insignificant fragments were found. I have already mentioned the indications of a gradual accumulation of earth that could be seen in the remains of the altar and the boundary walls of the temple precinct; but the facts now before us can be explained on no such hypothesis. It is, in the first place, all but impossible that such a thick accumulation of rubbish of all kinds should be allowed within the temenos. Then no stratification, chronological or other, can be observed within the layers; and no distinction in style or age of pottery and inscriptions can be drawn between the upper and lower layer. Again, fragments of the same vase or statuette were often found, some on the north, some on the south, some on the east of the temple. Such a scattering and confusion can hardly be explained by any other supposition than this; the contents of the first temple must have been violently broken and

---

[1] This north wing is hatched in Pl. I. as level 300—315; its foundation is really 7 inches higher; but it did not seem worth while to introduce a fresh notation for so small a difference, no others of less than twenty inches being indicated.

thrown out into the temenos around it. Mr. Petrie has suggested to me an ingenious explanation of the sand and the upper layer of fragments; perhaps when the second temple was to be built, the site was first artificially raised to the level of the surrounding district; then all fragments that had remained within the temple on its destruction were cast forth, and mixed with the highest stratum of the filling in. The only objection to this theory is to be found in the indications of gradual accumulation we have just seen in the case of the altar and the precinct walls. But both processes, both the gradual and the sudden filling up of the site, must be assumed to some degree in different parts. It is in any case probable that the precinct of a temple would be better preserved from gradual accumulation than the land surrounding it. For this accumulation arises mostly from the washing down of mud-brick walls—a process that would hardly be allowed free scope in such a place. The road that runs just in front shows by its regular stratification that it was constantly necessary to put on fresh materials, as the district beside it was thus gradually rising in level. As to the time when the first temple was destroyed and its contents scattered, no certain evidence can be produced. But it seems extremely probable that here, as in the temenos of Apollo, the Persian invasion marks the later limit of what is found, and that some calamity befell the city of Naukratis at that time from which it never completely recovered.

(37) The town did, however, recover to some extent, as is proved by clear enough indications both in this temenos of Aphrodite and in other parts of the site. Here, upon the top of the walls of the first building, partly perhaps ruined, certainly afterwards levelled for the purpose, a new temple was founded. This new temple was not of exactly the same dimensions as the old one, nor did it occupy exactly the same site.

Its length and breadth were both alike increased. Thus it projected both in front, towards the east, and more still behind, towards the west, beyond the lines of the original building. Though the breadth also was increased, the wall of the new temple was beyond that of the old one only on the north side; on the south it was a little within the old limit. This was doubtless in order to bring the temple nearer to the middle of its temenos; now that the walls had disappeared, there was no longer any reason to consult other considerations than those of symmetry. The division between the cella and the opisthodomus also underwent a modification. It was extant, when found, from the south wall to a point some two-thirds of the distance across the building, and there were no signs of a door in the middle; hence the door must probably have been close to the north wall, where it is marked in the plan. The outside wall seems to have been continuous all round the back of the temple, and so the doorway marked in the plan is in the only place where means of access to the opisthodomus can have existed. Parts of the plaster that had once covered the walls and floor of the second temple were still visible, both inside and outside the building. Upon the floor, in the south-west corner of the cella, were found some accumulations of rubbish, including a disc of gold, some fragments of bronze and iron ornaments or implements, and some pieces of blue paint, fallen from the walls.

It will be seen that the great altar was completely underground at the time when the second temple was built. Nor is there any sign that another permanent structure was built to take its place. This alteration seems to have involved some modification in the boundary wall on the east side of the temenos, two portions of which may be seen to belong to the same date as the walls of the second temple. One of these portions ends in a square pillar, which most probably formed one side of the gateway that led up to the temple during this period.

(38) The third temple, which rested [2] upon the walls of the second, differed in arrangement from its two predecessors; it only contained a single chamber, occupying the whole space within the outer walls. Thus its cella was larger than that of the two earlier temples, though its entire measurements are somewhat smaller than those of the second one; it is, indeed, intermediate between the second and first temples in size. Some pieces of wall to the west of the sacred precinct seem to belong to the same period as the third temple, but they are hardly massive enough to be a part of the boundary wall. At the back of the temple it is hard to say whether that boundary wall still existed, but on the north and south the earliest wall still rises here and there above the level of the ground on which the third temple was built.

In the temenos were found fragments of a plaster floor, some belonging, from their level, to the period of the second temple, some to that of the third. They seem to show that the ground all round the temple rose gradually, and that the floor of the temenos had to be repeatedly renewed. A gradual accumulation of the ground during the later period also is unmistakably shown by the road, which appears on the extreme east of the upper section in Pl. III. It consists entirely of uniformly stratified layers, and must constantly have been raised, in order to be kept at the same level as the district around it, which at every shower received a fresh deposit of mud washed down from the mud-brick walls of the houses.

(39) Now that we have reviewed successively the three temples of Aphrodite and their

appurtenances, it remains for us briefly to consider their relations to one another, especially from the chronological point of view. We have already seen reason for believing that the first temple of Aphrodite was among the earliest built at Naukratis. If we think of other periods that we know to have been marked by activity in the rebuilding of old sanctuaries and the founding of new ones, two occur apparently to us as the most prominent —the close of the fifth century, when the temple of Apollo was rebuilt and that of the Dioscuri was probably constructed in its present form; and the period of the earliest Ptolemies, when the great repairs and alterations in the Hellenion and its neighbourhood were made. These dates would then at once suggest themselves as probable for the foundations of the second and third temples respectively in the temenos of Aphrodite. And the relation of the various levels is at least not inconsistent with the suggestion. Even if the rate of accumulation in the temenos itself was not regular, that of the district around may well have been so, as is shown, for instance, by the road; and each temple would in all probability be adapted to the level of the ground around it at the time when it was built. Now at a rate of accumulation of about forty inches a century, we obtain an interval of about 200 years between the first and second temples, of 100 between the second and third. If, then, we assign the foundation of the first temple to about 600 B.C., that of the second to 400 B.C., and that of the third to 300 B.C., we shall probably not be very far wrong. Of course these dates must be regarded as only approximate; there are not sufficient data to preserve us from an error of a few years on the one side or the other; but they will be a help to our memory in the endeavour to realize the various periods through which the city and its temples have passed.

[2] On the N.E., the face of the wall of the third temple is continued in front of that of the second temple, and apparently below what was then the ground level; it is not easy to see the reason for this arrangement.

CHAPTER V.

POTTERY FROM THE TEMENOS OF APHRODITE.

(40) THE site upon which the pottery was discovered has been described in the last chapter; and upon the section, Pl. III., are marked the various strata in which it was found. The circumstances under which these numerous fragments of fine pottery and other objects once dedicated in the temple came to be buried in the place where they were found, have already received some discussion. A few words may be added as to the condition of the vases or of their fragments. All were completely broken to pieces, and the pieces were in almost every case scattered amongst all the other refuse over the whole surface of the temenos. Thus the fragments belonging to each individual vase could only be recovered by gradually sorting the whole mass according to style and fabric. Many of the vases possessed, fortunately, a sufficient individuality of treatment or colour to make it possible to recognize their pieces at a glance. But this was not always the case, and therefore a systematic sorting was necessary. By this process were separated more than 150 vases, each represented by a number of fragments varying from two or three to seventy or eighty; in this total fragments are not included that remain isolated, and are only of value as fragments. To take one or two examples: the large bowl represented on Pl. XI. 3, is made up of sixty or more pieces; the plate, 1 and 2 of Pl. XI., of 46; the bowl with a lotus pattern, Pl. VII. 5, of 47. These are instances taken quite at random, and are fairly representative of the condition in which all the vases were found. Fortunately the colouring has in most cases suffered but little, and thus it is possible to restore in imagination the appearance of these vases, though they are so much mutilated.

(41) The following classification of the various styles and fabrics of pottery found in the temenos of Aphrodite at Naukratis cannot claim to be exhaustive; if it were so, it would necessarily be so overloaded with detail as to miss its intention, which is to give a general outline of the various kinds of pottery and their distinctions and characteristics. Even in the classification as now given I fear that some assignments may seem somewhat arbitrary; I may even in some cases have been led by characteristics that are accidental and not essential to the vases in which they occur. But my divisions are at least the result of a long and careful study of the pottery brought from Naukratis, and a familiarity gained by constantly sorting and turning over the fragments; and the difficulty of my task must serve as an excuse for any errors or inadequacies that may occur in my attempt to carry it out. After so much apology, I will proceed at once to the classification itself, which may be followed more easily with the help of the table at the end of this chapter.

A. White-glaze type (Naukratite).

All examples of this class are distinguished by the pure creamy colour of their glaze, and also by its fragility; it will peel off in flakes; on this are painted ornamental designs in brown, varying to light red; purple and sometimes white touches are added in the more developed examples; once or twice, too, a pink flesh colour for the skin of men; as a rule, the drawing is in fine outline, and no incised lines are used; two exceptions will be noticed below.

a. Bowls of the shape indicated in Nauk. I. Pl. X. 1 and 3, a rounded body and a long conical rim, which is, indeed, the chief field for ornament. The body is decorated outside by plain brown bands, and at the top by a line of guillauche pattern. These vases are always black inside with lotus patterns, rosettes, &c., in red and white, varying in gorgeousness and complexity, but always of the same nature (see Nauk. I. Pl. V. 1—10. Journ. of Hell. Stud., 1887, Pl. LXXIX.). This ware is undoubtedly of local manufacture, as is proved not only by the quantity of it found here and nowhere else,[1] but by inscriptions painted on it before firing, showing it to have been specially made for dedication to Aphrodite.

1. Small, only ornamented with concentric bands and geometrical patterns; inside as described. (Nauk. I. Pl. V. 29, 30).

2. Usually somewhat larger, with animals and figures (Pl. V. 2—6; Nauk. I. Pl. V. 11—28). Style similar to next class.

3. Similar, but very fine; some examples must have been fourteen inches or more in diameter at the top when perfect. Thus they approximate to the ordinary crater in shape and size (Pl. V. 7; Journ. of Hell. Stud., 1887, Pl. LXXIX., where the inside and outside of one of the finest fragments are

[1] There are two small examples in the Louvre, from Rhodes; we might expect some exports thither, since so many vases were imported from that island.

excellently reproduced in the colours of the original). The empty spaces of the field are always varied, but not filled up, with geometrical and other ornaments. The colouring is wonderfully rich in its decorative effect. The drawing, on the other hand, though often very delicate and careful, seems to lack the vigour that marks some of the other types of pottery, and sometimes sinks to a purely conventional treatment. Thus muscles of animals tend to become meaningless spirals. So too the lion's head on Pl. V. 7, however fine, looks weak when contrasted with the powerful jaws of the beast on a different ware (B. b.) depicted also in Pl. LXXIX. of the Hellenic Journal. Yet for beauty and richness of decorative effect one can hardly deny that this white glazed ware surpasses all others. The easy freedom of the brush seems, however, to have enervated its art, while the concise vigour of the incised line has left more strength to the drawing which we shall meet in class B.

4. Similar to 2; but generally smaller; with incised lines. This treatment was especially used for grotesque figures of negroes, &c., (see Nauk. I. Pl. V. 34, 35, 40—42, &c.) If these figures have sometimes more rude vigour of drawing, they entirely lack the fineness and delicacy that marks classes 2 and 3. In one or two exceptional cases we find incised lines combined with careful colouring, e.g. in the dark red heads, Nauk. I. Pl. V. 35 (one or two other similar examples have been found).

A. b. Similar, but much larger and coarser vases; only a few fragments have been found, which are not sufficient to justify any conjecture as to their shape. The ground is again white; the drawings, often apparently of scenes of combat, including human figures, in brown outlines, with the use, sometimes, of pink flesh colour.

c. Small and delicate vases of various shapes, minute cups, &c. The ornamentation is similar to that of a 1 and 2.

d. This is one of the most magnificent examples of ancient pottery found at Naukratis; one complete bowl has been recovered, and there are fragments of a second (Pl. VI. two views). The bowl is of an open, basin-like shape; it has two triple handles, each terminating in a human face at each end; and between the handles on each side is a boss with two faces back to back. The glaze is a pure creamy white; the design in light red or brown, with touches of purple. The outline drawing is similar in style and execution to that which we meet in A.

b. This reason, as well as the fact that the glaze, colouring, and decorative effect are similar, lead me to assign this class to the type A. And it is hardly a rash conclusion that these bowls also are the work of the potters of Naukratis, and are among the masterpieces of their craft.

It is to be observed that the designs on the fragmentary bowl seem simpler than those on the complete one; and that the forms of the letters in its inscription of dedication are certainly earlier (see Pl. XXI. 701—705). It seems probable that it must have been an earlier experiment in the style of which we are fortunate enough to possess an almost perfect example in its later development: perhaps the

dedicators of the two are identical; but it is hardly probable that the dedicator was the potter himself, for he is most unlikely to have so disfigured his work by a carelessly incised inscription.

e. Similar ware, with designs of similar style, is also found in other shapes: of particularly delicate work is the askion represented in Pl. V. 1; we can hardly err in assigning this to the same local class of pottery.

f. Of open bowls, slightly narrowing towards the neck, and with a flat horizontal rim (the shape of the bowl represented on Pl. X.), some very fragmentary remains were found in this same white glazed ware; the colouring and drawing were similar to that of d; among the animals on it we may especially observe a leopard, drawn only in outline, and his spots indicated by circles in outline, —a good instance of the preference found in this style for outline work. On the horizontal rim is often a guillauche pattern—a favourite design throughout this type.

g. The next class bears a strong resemblance in many ways to a. 4, which we have already considered; its representative is the cover apparently of some vase, figured on Pl. VII. 2. This and a. 4 are distinguished from all other examples of this type by the use of incised lines. Together with them we also find a vigour and humour in the treatment of the subject represented, here sphinxes and lions; the little lion playing with the sphinx's tail can hardly be anything but a humorous touch. In this example the material seems closer and the glaze more durable than in most other specimens of this pottery; but the style and effect will hardly allow us to separate it from our present type.

h. Lamps (Pl. VII. 3). Several lamps of this peculiar shape and construction were found: the example selected might almost as well be assigned to some other type; but since one specimen shows the characteristic white glaze and guilloche pattern, it must certainly be assigned its place here; and it seems convenient not to separate these peculiar lamps from one another. These lamps show no sign of use, and may have been purely ornamental; it may even be disputed if they are lamps at all, but such seems the most probable intention to ascribe to their shape. We may most suitably mention here a bowl with a round bottom and horizontal rim, ornamented only with parallel bands of red on a whitish ground; on the brim is a pattern of cross lines, as on the "lamp" in the plate. The two handles are made of triple rings.

B. Eye-bowl type (Naukratite). This type is characterized by the decoration of the interior of the broad basin-like bowls that it comprises. This is in every case, from the smallest and most insignificant to the largest and most sumptuous specimens, precisely similar—only in a few examples further ornamentation is added; but we never miss the essential part. The whole inside of the bowls is covered with a hard and brilliant glaze, varying according to the firing from red to dark brown in colour, but very different from the dull black of type A. Unlike that, again, it is very durable, and never peels off. On this glaze are painted parallel bands in red or purple and white, at regular intervals from the centre to the edge. The glaze of the outside is of a brownish-yellow colour, only approaching in a few specimens the whiteness of type A.; it also is quite fast, and never peels off the surface of the vase. In the ornamentation of this outside we may distinguish various classes.

a. The eye-bowl proper, so called from the frequent occurrence on vases of this type of a large pair of eyes, often with a conventional arrangement of spirals between them to represent a nose.

1. The shapes may be seen in Nauk. I. Pl. X. 11. Another common ornament is a set of vertical lines close together (as in the specimen referred to).

2. Similar, but of more complex shape, with double or triple brim, and four handles, one above another on each side (Pl. VII. 1). It is not impossible this vase may be a mere accident, or a caprice of the potter's, who made two of these vases into one. In any case it is of great interest as bearing the dedication of the sculptor Rhœcus to Aphrodite; a part of this may be seen near the bottom of the vase in the illustration (see also Pl. XXI. 778).

b. 1. A splendid series of large bowls was found which one might not, at first glance, be inclined to connect with this type. But the similar treatment of the interior seems to indicate that we have here a development, far indeed removed from the simple original from which it is derived, but preserving the essential characteristics of the type. These bowls are decorated with friezes, partly of animals, partly of vegetable or merely geometrical forms. The lotus is an especial favourite; of this a very graceful variety, combined with an inverted palmetto, may be seen on Pl. VII. 5.

F

The peculiar combination of spiral volute and lotus which may be seen beside the handle of all these bowls was even last year described by Mr. Petrie as especially belonging to Naukratis. For last year many fragments of these bowls were discovered (Nauk. I. Pl. VI. 3—5, XIII. 2, 3). The animals represented are lions, leopards, boars, stags, ibexes, and birds; sphinxes and human-headed birds (called harpies or sirens in later applications of the form) also occur. For style the best examples are Pl. IX. 1. (which though belonging to the next class, is similar to this outside), and the bowl reproduced in the original colours on Pl. LXXIX. of the Hellenic Journal. The two lions and the stag between them on that plate are a very powerful piece of drawing and composition; though there may be errors, as in the foreleg of the stag, there is a vigour and force in the conception and execution which forms a great contrast to the delicate but conventional work of type A. And it is a fact not unconnected with the style, that incised lines are always used in the drawing of animals on the upper frieze of these vases, though never upon the purely decorative and ornamental designs that occur in the lower ones, even though these include ibexes.

Fortunately we possess a clear proof that these large bowls are the work of local artists. On one of them is an inscription, painted before firing in large white letters on the dark glaze inside the rim, recording its dedication to "the Aphrodite at Naukratis" (Pl. XXI. 768). It therefore follows that to type B., as well as

to type A., we must assign a local origin; they seem to show the development of two simple indigenous styles of fabric and decoration; this conclusion is strongly confirmed by the fact that neither type was known [2] before the excavations at Naukratis, and that to the two belong the greater number of all the fine vases found on the site.

2. This differs only from 1 in the richness of the interior decoration, which is represented on Pl. VIII. 2. The principal designs are again drawn from the lotus; between them are sets of vertical bars which again recall the ornamentation on the outside of the eye-bowls, and so afford a further confirmation of identity of type in all these bowls, from the smallest to the largest. The bowl on Pl. VIII. is no less than twenty inches in diameter, without including the handles.

C. Black and red [3] type. Here we descend at once from the new and characteristic vases of Naukratis to those which it exhibits in common with all other Greek sites. Some examples may call for special notice; but there is no reason here for assuming any peculiar local manufacture.

a. Simple bowls, usually of the cylix shape.
1. Plain.
2. Decorated with a series of concentric bands inside, of black and red alter-

---

[2] See, however, the exception mentioned under type A, p. 39.

[3] I use the word "red" here in preference to "buff," which is used by Mr. Petrie to denote the same colour in Nauk. I., because the names "black-figured" and "red-figured" vases are terms of universal use and acceptation. It must be borne in mind that when I speak here of "black and red" vases, I mean precisely the same as Mr. Petrie when he speaks of "black and buff."

nating. The bands vary in width
from an inch or more to the finest
lines that can be drawn; sometimes
they are on all except the rim, sometimes on the rim only.

3. The rim decorated outside with a continuous wreath, usually of olive, in
black on the red ground.

4. Various other decorations; among the
most peculiar are small applied astra-
gali and ram's heads (Nauk. I. Pl.
XIII. 1).

b. Painted with various animals and human
figures, in black on the red ground, in
friezes round the vase; touched with
purple and sometimes with white. Of
this almost universally found type of
pottery two classes are worth especial
mention.

1. Bowls with a flat horizontal rim, usually
with no stand, but a spherical bottom;
the rim decorated with rosettes. (Pl.
IX. 6, 7.) The subjects are men,
human-headed birds, leopards, boars,
&c. Incised lines are used; the field
is left quite plain. The man holding
a staff or caduceus, facing one of the
human-headed birds, is interesting, as
an example of the probable prototype
of the group later appropriated to the
scene of Œdipus and the Sphinx.
Harpy, Sphinx, and Siren had not probably yet assumed the distinct forms
in which they are known to later art.
Those forms are certainly unknown to
early mythology.

2. This class is similar to the last, but
that the vases it contains are jugs, of
the œnochoe shape, and not bowls: the
friezes of animals are of a similar
nature in both cases.

c. Of the same colours, but larger and
coarser, and with designs also of a
larger and rougher style. The design

is usually in black on a square red panel
left clear of the black ground; the vases
are sometimes large bowls, sometimes
jugs (Pl. XIII. 2; IX. 5, with a large
ram; this comes from the bottom of one
of the wells; cf. Nauk. I. Pl. VI. 1, 2,
also from the bottom of a well—a likely
place to find jugs).

d. Small and delicate vases, often of extreme
beauty in detail (VII. 4; IX. 8). No
further classification of these seems to
be of much use. The examples given
will speak for themselves, especially the
first.

Throughout, in speaking of a type so common
as this, I have made no attempt at an exhaustive
enumeration, but have merely selected a few
interesting or peculiar examples.

D. Geometrical, of very early style. One example of this was found at the bottom of
a well; it was a large jug or hydria, of
light-grey ware, with only the simplest
ornentation in cross-lines in light red.
Being of rough and coarse ware, it may
well have been used for ordinary purposes. But in any case the appearance of
a vase of so primitive a character among
fine Greek pottery calls for some comment; it would seem to show that such
articles may have survived for ordinary
rough use, side by side with the more
artistic productions of the Greek potters.

E. 1. Cyrenaic. Several specimens of this ware
have been found at Naukratis during
both the seasons of excavation: most
noteworthy is the splendid bowl reproduced by Mr. Petrie on Pl. VIII
and IX. of Naukratis I; another piece
is figured in the same volume, Pl. VII.
11, and two or three other vases, more
or less fragmentary, were found in the
temenos of Aphrodite. In Naukratis
1. p. 53, Mr. Cecil Smith made the

F 2

suggestion that it was not impossible that this peculiar style of pottery should be attributed, not to Cyrene, but to Naukratis.[*] But he did not then think there was sufficient evidence to justify our setting aside the accepted name and attribution; and we certainly have not now any more reason for rejecting it. The peculiar fabric of these vases, and the style of their decoration, are not at all similar in their nature to those we find upon the vases that we know now to have been made at Naukratis itself. The Cyrenaic ware is so peculiar, that any fragment of it can at a glance be picked out from the confused mass; yet the total number recovered does not imply the existence of more than three or four vases in the temenos of Aphrodite—an impossibly small number, if the ware were really of local manufacture. On two of the Cyrenaic vases were inscriptions (Pl. XXI. 766—767); on one was the name Negomandrus, on the other, probably, Philammon. This last is a name that is obviously fitting for a Cyrenean, when we remember the close relations between Cyrene and the cult of Zeus Ammon,—

> " Oraclum Jovis inter æstuosi
> Et Batti veteris sacrum sepulcrum."

Negomandrus also has a Græco-Egyptian look about it, that seems to imply a connection with either Naukratis or Cyrene : in several cases besides this there is good reason for supposing that it was customary for dedicators to offer the ware that was

made at their native cities. On the whole, then, while we have no farther reason for connecting this " Cyrenaic " ware with Naukratis, but rather evidence for rejecting such a connection, further confirmation is given to the theory which attributes its origin to Cyrene.

F. Flat, plate-like, shapes. To make a class like this dependent apparently upon the shape rather than the fabric or style of the pottery, may seem inconsistent; but the vases comprised in it will be found, for the most part, to have some characteristic in common besides their form.

a. Slightly curving up towards the rim with or without stands (Pinaces).

  1. Decorated only with lines, or with vegetable forms, especially lotus ; occasionally with a head of an animal in a square, among other decorative designs—the ordinary Asia Minor and Rhodian type; red on light yellow, often with purple touches (Nauk. I. Pl. VII. 1—6.)

  2. Much richer in decoration; especially in one very fine example, painted both sides, with concentric friezes of animals, boars, leopards, ibexes, birds, and sphinxes : a very rich lotus pattern is also added. The style of this plate recalls that of some of the finest Naukratite vases, and suggests that this also may have been made in the town (Pl. IX. 1—4 both sides of the same plate).

b. The field quite flat, surrounded by a raised edge, which serves also as a frame to the designs.

  1. Plain.

  2. With various designs, mostly representing animals, usually arranged in concentric friezes ; various fabrics and colours are found, sometimes the

---

[*] I am sorry to see that this suggestion, which Mr. Smith himself would not now maintain, has been repeated with confidence in the continuation of M. Dumont's work, " Les Céramiques de la Grèce propre." See below, p. 51.

ordinary black and red, sometimes red figures on a whitish ground, sometimes a very fine white pottery, from which the ornamentation has almost entirely disappeared.

3. With human figures; brown on a white ground with purple touches: incised lines are used (Pl. XI. 1, 2). The figures are arranged in concentric friezes, and there are a few beasts, perhaps lions, as well as men. The dress of the men is very peculiar, apparently a mere loin-cloth closely tied in. The whole treatment seems to be more or less humorous, thus one of the men grasps the tail of a lion, which being by the design inverted, presents an incoherent effect. We may indeed compare this plate, though its execution is far superior, with the humorous figures which we met with in class A. a. 4. And, both in colouring and design, it resembles strongly the local pottery of Naukratis. It is also similar to a neck of a large vase with a row of dancing female figures (Pl. XIII. 1), which seems to be of the same fabric (see type H. b.)

4. In some cases the field is not divided into concentric bands, but is treated as a whole; in that case the lower portion is sometimes cut off, as the exergue of a coin, and filled with a subsidiary design or merely with ornamentation. A very curious example of this may be seen on Pl. XX., where the fantastic beasts in various positions occupy both parts of the field. But by far the finest specimen discovered was the plate with a single figure of a seated sphinx, Pl. XII. This is a plaque painting rather than a vase design. It is executed with the utmost delicacy and ease, in four

colours—yellow, brown, purple or red, and white; these are the typical four colours of early painting, and we can hardly doubt that they were the four that characterized the technique of Polygnotus and other early masters. Here, then, we have an example closely approaching to a panel picture, showing us exactly how those colours were used. Perhaps the most remarkable thing of all is the use of touches of white to bring out the high lights. Unfortunately it is hardly possible to see this now, but when the plate was first taken out of the ground, such touches were distinctly visible in some places, especially on the front of the fore-legs and paws. The use of the other colours may be pretty clearly seen on the plate. The outlines are drawn in brown with a brush, but incised lines are also used, especially to indicate the plumage on the breast. Above the head of the sphinx two small holes were bored through the rim of the plate, clearly indicating that it was intended to be hung up, in all probability as a picture to decorate the wall of the temple. If so, we may with yet more certainty regard this plaque as affording us invaluable information as to the style prevalent in the free paintings of the period—if indeed any existed in the sixth century which were not purely decorative in their subject and treatment.

G. Ibex type. This title is in many respects unsatisfactory; on some of the vases included under it the ibex is not found; and the ibex often occurs on other pottery which, though somewhat similar, has elsewhere been classified. But the animal is of such frequent occurrence on this type of ware that it seems to afford a characteristic mark by which we may indicate it. The ground is always yellow, the design is light red, shading to brown, sometimes with touches of purple. Sometimes examples of this ware approach very closely to A e and other classes, but the drawing seldom shows the same delicacy and finish. The origin of this pottery is very probably Rhodian; it was well enough known before it was found at Naukratis; there is one very fine example, a jug, in the Museum at Bulak (cf. Pl. XIII. 3). The friezes of animals of this type of pottery are almost precisely similar to the lower friezes upon the large bowls, type B; both are without incised lines, and so have outline drawing extensively used.

a. With tiers of ibexes (Pl. XIII. 3); this I regard as the typical form. This jug also comes from a well in the temenos; hence it appears that it, as well as that previously mentioned, was for actual use, not only for ornament.

b. The covers of some vessels ornamented with the same animal. These covers are also found with the common ornamentation of Rhodian pinakes. Hence again it would appear that this type has its home in Rhodes.

11. Large bowls, with a flat horizontal rim; the ground light yellow or whitish, the designs in red varying to dark brown, according to the firing.

a. With friezes of animals (Pl. X.); these are often arranged into splendid groups in the most conspicuous positions; for instance, the serpent and the two cocks on the vase reproduced; on the other side are two horsemen facing one another, an eagle flying between them.

The lower frieze is merely a consecutive band of animals, mostly leopards and stags. Incised lines are used, but the slight lines visible round the contours of the horse on the left are only added in the plate, as the outline is very indistinct upon the vase. This is a type of vase of which I believe this one from Naukratis is the first example to reach the British Museum; but the Louvre already possesses a fairly numerous series. These vases are exhibited in Room 5 of the Musée Campana; and are described as "vases of Corinthian origin from Etruria." On some of the later examples inscriptions in the Corinthian alphabet confirm this attribution. Some are precisely similar to the bowl on our Pl. X.; one has two cocks and a serpent, another two horsemen and a bird, just as this. The subjects are various, friezes of animals and men, scenes from life, banquets, &c., on the upper part, rows of animals below. This series almost merges in its latest examples into the ordinary black and red type. The field is rarely quite free from ornaments till the latest period; in this particular our vase is distinguished from them. It certainly in style and covering ranks among the earlier examples of the series; and of these it is perhaps the finest, though it has been so much broken. The inscription recording its dedication by Philis adds to its interest (Pl. XXI. 780).

b. Larger, and richer in colouring, white and purple being freely used (Pl. XI. 3). This vase was nearly two feet in diameter. The animals, which are very bold and vigorous in their drawing, are lions, bulls, ibexes, human-headed birds, &c. Here, as in class B, the upper friezes have incised lines; the lower and subordinate ones, of ibexes only, have none; this affords an argument for the vase being of local fabric. The handles are very peculiar in their arrangement, owing doubtless to the enormous weight and size of the vase they had to support. Similar in colouring, though not in size, and even more interesting in subject, is the neck with a series of dancing women (Pl. XIII. 1). The drawing of these figures is in some respects like that of the dancing men on the large flat plate (Pl. XI. 1, 2), but the vase seems best to find its place here. But I am inclined to think it probable that both this class H. b. and also F. b. 3, were made at Naukratis; the glaze on both resembles that on type A, which is undoubtedly local.

I. A very fine and soft whitish-yellow pottery, with simple ornaments in a bright red glaze. The best specimen is a jug from well 1. The neck was red, and there was red ornamentation round its base, and also the base of the jug. The jug is also remarkable for being circular in the neck, not of the usual trefoil shape. The triple handle was very delicate, made of three pieces, which had broken off, and were each separately recovered. Similar to this jug in fabric and ornamentation was a small urn which was found in the cemetery—apparently containing ashes.

J. Here also may be mentioned, though the shape of the vase from which they come is not clear, some peculiar fragments. In these the ground is a black glaze, laid over ordinary red pottery, and the design, whether of plant or animal forms, is painted on this ground in white. Unfortunately it is impossible to add much

more to this brief statement, as the fragments found were very few, and in very bad condition. A large vase, decorated in a similar manner, may be seen in the British Museum; it can only be distinguished from "Polledrara" ware by careful examination.

K. Black throughout, through the whole fabric of the ware, glazed or highly polished outside.

a. Bowls with a horizontal rim (shape, probably, as in Pl. IX. 6).

b. Large conical stands, with raised bands round the base.

c. Tripods and other ornamental pieces, with relief ornamentation.

d. Various small bowls, plates, &c.

This black ware is of especial interest from the inscriptions that were found on it. (Pl. XXI. 786—793; cf. also Pl. XXII. 840). As will be seen from the remarks on those inscriptions in Chapter VIII., it is extremely probable that they all record dedications by Mytileneans or Lesbians. If that be the case, it is hardly rash to assume that the ware which they so consistently dedicated was a product of their native island. This is an assumption which can only be tested by excavation in Lesbos itself; meanwhile we may hope that we have learnt something as to both the pottery and the alphabet that belonged to the island of Sappho. This black ware, as has been pointed out by Mr. Cecil Smith, is similar to the "Polledrara" ware from Rhodes. But the "Polledrara" ware has not been found there in sufficient quantity to prove it a local fabric; in both places it may be imported from Lesbos, Mr. Smith tells me he has found traces of colour on the black ground on this, as on the "Polledrara" ware; but

I have not detected them; compare type J, and see below p. 51.

L. Dark rough earthenware, with a greenish glaze. One small bowl of this nature was found; it probably is not of Greek make.

M. Rough, unpainted pottery. This was of various shapes, mostly adapted to use; bowls, cups, plates, &c.; but no specimens seem to call for any especial comment except the lamps. Beside the ordinary types described by Mr. Petrie last year (Nauk. I. p. 45), were found several which must have had a very large number of wicks, and one of a peculiar construction. This was a shallow, circular dish, enclosing an open space in the middle; round both the inner and the outer edge of the circular trough thus formed were a very large number of small holes pierced through an overhanging brim, in such a way as to support a continuous series of wicks round both margins. I have seen a similar arrangement in a lamp preserved in the Acropolis Museum at Athens. Other specimens of the pottery discovered might here be quoted, but they would perhaps overweight an enumeration already sufficiently complicated.

(42) We have now considered in detail the various types of pottery that are found at Naukratis, and especially in the temenos of Aphrodite. We have seen which of them are probably, which certainly, the work of the potters for whom the city was famous. A few words must now be added as to the relation of these types, not only to one another, but also to other kinds of pottery that are found upon early Hellenic sites; and also as to the probable age of the pottery discovered at Naukratis. Fortunately the first of these questions has

already been considered by Mr. Cecil Smith, in his chapter on the pottery in Naukratis I. But the far more complete and representative series of pottery from Naukratis that we now possess has supplied fuller material than was available for his discussion of the subject. In a subject so extremely complicated as that of the early history of vase-painting, it will be best, before we venture on any general sketch, to notice a few points that seem to throw light upon some difficult problems. It will already have been observed by those who remember the distinction noticed by Mr. Cecil Smith (Nauk. I. p. 50) between what he then termed the "Assyrian" and the "Egyptian" classes of the "Oriental" style of vase-painting, that our type A roughly corresponds to the latter, B to the former. In the "Egyptian" class Mr. Smith observes that "no incised lines are used, and the artist is in consequence forced to leave portions of his figure in outline." This is just the characteristic that we observed in class A, the white glazed Naukratite vases. In class B, on the other hand, which, as we have seen, is also of local manufacture, we always find incised lines, and what seems to be a development of the "Assyrian"[5] style of vase-painting, in the principal friezes; but in the subordinate or merely ornamental parts we have no incised lines; sometimes we have decorative friezes of ibexes, on the lower and less seen parts of the bowls (Pl. VIII. cf. also Pl. XI. 3), which recall at once Mr. Smith's "Egyptian style." Thus these bowls offer at once a striking analogy to the vase published by him in the Hellenic Journal, VI., p. 186, with its two friezes in the two different styles; and thus we have a confirmation of his view that such

[5] I have adopted here Mr. Cecil Smith's terms; the nomenclature of this subject is already sufficiently confusing. Mr. Smith's terms are, however, only used "for convenience," and he probably would not insist on their scientific accuracy. "Dorian" is by Mr. Murray used as equivalent to "Egyptian" in this context, as Mr. Smith points out—a good illustration of the uncertainty of the subject.

vases must be attributed to Naukratis. In any case it is clear that Naukratis was not a centre of exclusively Egyptian influence upon the early art of Greece. We must rather believe that in this colony the Greeks found many channels by which they derived the technique and subjects of their representations from various Eastern sources. Through their intercourse with the Phœnicians, whom they must have constantly met in their coasting voyages and especially in Cyprus, they must have felt the influence of Assyria as well as that of Egypt upon their art. Here, as in other cases, we shall not find them ready to borrow much directly from the ancient and stereotyped art of Egypt.

Rhodes afforded still earlier a great centre of Greek and Phœnician intercourse. The influence of Rhodes upon Naukratis is very great. Rhodian pottery is constantly found in the Egyptian colony; and it is often extremely hard to say whether a vase is a product of the local potteries, or an import from Rhodes. But Naukratis is far freer alike in subject and in style; and we certainly find here a variety and an advance in artistic invention and execution which would make it an easy task to select the masterpieces of the potteries of Naukratis from among a number of other products of the earliest Greek vase-painters.

As regards the period to which we must assign the vases found in the temenos of Aphrodite, it is not easy to come to a definite decision. But one thing is clear; we have here no stratification, no gradual accumulation that began at one time, and ended perhaps a century and a half later. All these fragments of vases and statuettes must have been cast forth at the same time; though of course they may have gradually been accumulating in the temple from which they came. Many of the vases and of the inscriptions which they bear seem to belong to the same period as the later vases from the temenos of Apollo; that is to say, to

the latter half of the sixth century B.C. As has already been observed, all the circumstances seem to point to a violent destruction of the temple and its contents, and such a destruction is very likely to have taken place, in this temenos as well as in that of Apollo, at the time of the Persian invasion. If thus we suppose that the vases which have been discovered were for the most part made and dedicated during the half century which preceded the year 520 B.C., we probably shall not be far from the truth. And this conclusion, though it lacks the clearness of successive periods that could be attained in the temenos of Apollo, may yet be of great value to us in showing what styles of pottery were contemporary, and in fixing approximately the date to which they must be assigned.

We must now make some attempt to estimate the position of Naukratis in the early history of Greek vase painting. We have here a dated series; and we may divide the early Greek pottery as to which we may hope to learn something, into three classes. Firstly, we may consider such pottery as is absent from Naukratis, for this absence is in itself an important indication; it implies that the types of pottery in question either were not being made at the time when this accumulation at Naukratis was taking place, or were by some reason prevented from coming in any quantity to Naukratis. In the second place, we may discuss those types found at Naukratis which we know to have been made elsewhere, and to have been previously found upon other sites; for we now have data for assigning a fairly definite and certain period to their manufacture. Then lastly must be mentioned those vases that seem to have been made at Naukratis itself, whether scattered examples have found their way by export to other sites, or we find in them types new to the student of Greek pottery.

It is of course not necessary to enumerate all the primitive types of pottery found upon

Greek soil, in speaking of those that are absent from Naukratis. That absence only becomes interesting when we reach the products of a period not far removed from those at which the temples of Naukratis flourished. Of Mycenæ vases we of course expect and find nothing : and the geometrical style that follows them or is contemporaneous with them in Greece and the islands (" Dipylon " and " Island " style) also lacks any characteristic representative. But here the absence is not quite complete. A vase from a well in the temenos of Aphrodite, with a decoration of crossed lines (Type D), cannot fairly be quoted. It is quite isolated, and may perhaps be an importation from Cyprus, where this style of work lingered later than in Greece. But upon bowls of the eye-bowl class (Type B a. 1.), we sometimes meet with birds in the panels between the groups of vertical lines almost precisely similar to those we find in the interstices of the geometrical patterns on the " Dipylon" and " Island" vases. Mr. Cecil Smith[6] is doubtless right in describing these " brown bowls " as " evidently imitations of the 'Geometric' style made much later than the archaic period to which they probably belong;" but the mere survival of such forms is of itself enough to show that the interval in time between the two classes is not very great, or at least that no other different types intervened. For of course at such a period there is no question of conscious antiquarian imitation of earlier ware. We may then definitely fix the period of geometrical ornamentation as preceding, but immediately preceding, the accumulation of vases in the temples at Naukratis ; and if we assign that accumulation to the sixth century, the later varieties of the geometrical style will find their place in the seventh. And when we remember that a geometric vase now in the Polytechnic Museum at Athens bears the earliest Attic inscription in-

scribed upon it, we shall hardly be disposed to carry the latest examples of that style beyond the seventh century, for as yet we have no reason for assuming the use of the alphabet in Greece during the eighth century. All our facts indeed point to its being still in the transition of adaptation during the earlier part of the seventh century. The result, then, which we obtain in this case from the evidence of excavation is in accordance with our expectations, and affords a satisfactory confirmation to the dates we are otherwise led to assign to certain types of Archaic Greek pottery.

We must next consider those types of pottery that, though probably made elsewhere, have been found at Naukratis. For we may now go on with some confidence, and assign them to the sixth century. Some of course may only have survived into this period, others may have only begun during its lapse a development to be carried farther in later times: of others, again, it may have contained both the rise and the decline. We need not spend much time over all these types of vases ; a mere glance at the table at the end of this chapter will suffice to show what they are. But one or two styles call for more notice, either because we have now something more to say about their origin, or because some misunderstandings have arisen as to their relation to Naukratis. These styles are the Lesbian, the Cyrenaic, and the Rhodian ; they have already been mentioned in the classification of the pottery, but it seemed better to reserve for this place a somewhat fuller discussion of the questions to which they give rise.

In Naukratis, Part I.,[7] are mentioned certain fragments in which the clay is black throughout; many more fragments of this ware and some almost perfect vessels were found in the temenos of Aphrodite (Type K). But an important difference must be mentioned ; the fragments found in the temenos of Apollo had decorations in "a rich red colour" and others still visible upon the black ground; but those found in the temenos of Aphrodite were mostly plain, and in no case were the traces of colour distinct, though Mr. Cecil Smith tells me he has succeeded in discovering them in one or two instances. It is probable, however, that in any case the pottery is of the same type, and that it is hardly to be separated from a similar ware found in Rhodes, and called by Mr. Smith "Polledrara" ware, because the finest example of black painted ware is a hydria in the British Museum from a tomb at Polledrara. But the style of that hydria seems to be distinctly Etruscan, and to prove a local origin, the ware being the common Etruscan black fabric. If so, I am hardly disposed to adopt this name for the pottery of Rhodes and Naukratis.

I have already given reasons which seem almost convincing, for believing that the black pottery found at Naukratis was made in Lesbos. The question arises whether we must suppose that the specimens found in Rhodes were also imported from Lesbos, or that the theory of Lesbian origin is in all cases a mistake, or that there were in early times two factories, one in Rhodes and one in Lesbos. I incline to the first of these three suppositions; for I do not think the evidence for a Rhodian origin is strong enough to outweigh that of the Lesbian dedications; nor on the other hand is it probable that there were two distinct factories for a ware so different from any other known in this region and period. We may then, until we acquire farther evidence such as could best be supplied by excavations on Lesbos itself, regard this black pottery as a fabric peculiar to that island in the sixth century.

The next class with which we have to deal will present more difficulties. It is commonly known as Cyrenaic, and I do not believe that we have any reason for abandoning that name. Such new evidence as we possess tends rather to confirm it, as has already been pointed out

in our classification (Type E). But it calls for especial attention both because of the suggestion already referred to, that it was made at Naukratis; and also because of certain misapprehensions that have arisen from its apparent similarity to the characteristic Naukratite ware, our type A. Since the collection and comparison of known examples made by Dr. Puchstein in the "Archæologische Zeitung" of 1881, this style has attracted considerable notice; and we may in the first place notice that its occurrence at Naukratis is what we might expect from its usually accepted period, the middle of the sixth century B.C. But it is not found in any great profusion. Mr. Petrie discovered one nearly complete example, and four or five others more or less fragmentary have since appeared. These, however, are no more than one would expect to find in a colony so near Cyrene, if the ware were Cyrenaic; on the other hand, they are far too small a number to find if we had really discovered the place where this pottery was made; for at least thirty examples had already been found on other sites. The fact is that a misapprehension has arisen in some quarters, which is not unnatural in any who have only read descriptions of one of the two kinds of ware, but would at once be corrected by an examination of the vases themselves. All students of vases are now familiar with the characteristics of Cyrenaic ware; the usual, though not invariable, cylix shape, the hard and brilliant white glaze, the peculiar palmettos on the outside, the close and elaborate lotus and pomegranate patterns, the rich metallic ornateness of the whole effect, the frequent figure subjects. Now we do not meet with a single one of these characteristics upon our true Naukratite white-glazed ware. Here the shape is usually that of a diminutive crater with conical base, bowl-like body, and high conical rim, the chief field for painting; the glaze is flaky and crumbling, and of a dead-white colour outside; inside it is a dull black; the decorative patterns introduced show great variety in the outside borders, mostly of guillauche or maeander; inside they are of lotus, in red and white on the black ground, but freely and largely drawn, not closely set together; the whole effect is rich indeed, but with the richness of its colouring, the designs being always sparse and flowing; and the subjects are always animals, more or less decoratively treated.[6] The only resemblance between the two wares lies in the similarity of colouring, brown and red upon a whitish ground. But I venture to think that no fairly trained student of pottery would ever mistake even a minute fragment of white Naukratite ware for Cyrenaic; and this distinction of style sums up and is beyond all the detailed differences above enumerated.

We may then dismiss at once the view that the Cyrenaic and white-glazed Naukratite are only variations of the same type of pottery. But one supposition still remains possible. We have seen that two types so distinct as our A and B were both undoubtedly of local manufacture. May we believe that this "Cyrenaic" ware, though a different fabric, was also made at Naukratis? I think that we must answer this question in the negative, for the reason I have mentioned above, the small proportion borne by the specimens discovered at Naukratis to the total number known. Till excavations can be made at Cyrene—perhaps the most difficult and most promising site still waiting to be thoroughly explored—we cannot finally determine that the name Cyrenaic is correct; but in any case there is no reason for confusing

our nomenclature and our ideas by regarding this ware as another type of Naukratite pottery.[5]

A few words must suffice here for the Rhodian pottery, or Camirus style, as it is sometimes called.

This type (G) is often very difficult to distinguish from the white-glazed Naukratite (type A). This difficulty is what we should expect, if, as has already been stated, the influence of this Rhodian style was paramount in the workshops of Naukratis. I have already touched upon the difference between the two, which lies mostly in a certain refinement and delicacy of style that may be recognized with the eye more easily than described.

The mention of the Rhodian pottery, of which that of Naukratis seems to be a development, leads us on to the last question here to be considered : the position of Naukratis in the history of Greek vase-painting. Here, of course, I would speak only of those types of pottery which were without doubt made upon the spot. It is only in very few respects that these form a link in the regular succession of development, joined to other derived types that follow, as well as to the earlier styles from which they originate. Mr. Cecil Smith[1] has already suggested that we must regard the vases with black figures on a white ground as probably due originally to the influence of Naukratis, and has assigned a similar origin to certain other characteristics associated with the name of the artist Nikosthenes. But in any case this influence only affects some details of ornament or technique; it can hardly be traced in the style and character of the vases in question. On some sites[2] again have been found later vases with an internal ornamentation of white and sometimes

[6] It is necessary to dwell upon a distinction apparently so obvious, because the two are treated as similar, if not identical, in so valuable a work as Dumont and Chaplain's "Céramiques de la Grèce propre." This portion, written after M. Dumont's lamented death, is the work of M. Pottier, who gathers his information from the descriptions of Mr. Petrie and Mr. Cecil Smith. Doubtless he would have written differently had he been able to examine the Naukratite ware himself.

[5] In confirmation of the above views, it may be added that some fragments have been found at Naukratis which seem to be a local imitation of Cyrenaic pottery.
[1] Nauk. I. pp. 51, 52.
[2] E. g. on the Acropolis at Athens.

red also on a dark ground, that must be derived from Naukratis. This is, however, again only an isolated trait. On the whole, we must acknowledge that the pottery of Naukratis does not so much represent a stage in that transition from Oriental to purely Hellenic forms which is really the main subject of the early history of Greek ceramic art, as the most perfect and complete development of the decorative "oriental" style. From it we may learn what this style would become in the hands of artists who were gifted with an exquisite delicacy of touch, and a wonderful feeling for colour and decorative effect, but who lacked that freshness and originality both of conception and execution without which Greece would only have imitated and carried to that perfection of which it was capable the art inherited from the East. We see at Naukratis a style of vase-painting not only beautiful in itself—far more beautiful than the uncouth attempts at originality that were later to produce such wonderful results—but also interesting alike in what it attains and in what it lacks. Had all Greek art of the same period been like that of the Naukratite pottery, we should indeed possess many attractive works of a time that now has given to us more that we can find interesting for its promise than admire for its intrinsic beauty; but, on the other hand, without the originality that we here miss, the art of the sixth century could only have refined itself away into decorative detail in the fifth, instead of developing into the greatest that the world had ever seen. We may then be thankful for what is left us of the masterpieces of Naukratite pottery; but we must also be thankful that they are not fairly representative of all the tendencies of Greek art during the period to which they belong.

(For Table of Pottery, see next page.)

TABLE OF CLASSIFICATION OF POTTERY.

(43) ALL that has been said as to the circumstances under which the fragments of pottery were discovered in the temenos of Aphrodite applies equally to the statuettes. These were scattered about in quite as much confusion as the vases themselves, though, from the nature of their material, they were not broken into so many fragments. But portions of the same figure were often found in distant parts of the sacred precinct. The statuettes show even more indications than the vases of an intentional destruction; almost all the fractures, upon careful examination, show some signs of a severe blow upon one side. Hence it appears that they must have been violently broken up and then scattered—and by some enemy not only of the Greeks, but also of their religion. Such a proceeding is in accordance with what we know of the Persians; and hence yet further confirmation is gained by the conjecture, already well-founded, that it was the Persian invasion that led to a destruction of the temples at Naukratis, and gave a serious check to the prosperity of the city.

(44) But at present we are not concerned with the destruction of the statuettes, but with their origin, and with the history and progress of the art that produced them. And it will be well at this point to quote a passage of Athenæus, already referred to more than once, which has a direct bearing upon the origin of the statuettes discovered in the temenos of Aphrodite at Naukratis. Athenæus, himself a native of Naukratis, quotes from a work of his fellow-citizen Polycharmus, "On Aphrodite," the following story. "In the twenty-third olympiad, Herostratus, a fellow-citizen of ours, was on a journey; and having sailed round many lands, he touched also at Paphos in Cyprus; there he bought a statuette of Aphrodite, a span high, of archaic style, and went off with it to Naukratis. Now, when his ship was near Egypt, a storm suddenly came on, and they could not see whereabouts they were; so all of them took refuge by the image of Aphrodite, praying her to save them. And the goddess, with her wonted favour to the people of Naukratis, suddenly filled all the region about her with green myrtle, and made the ship full of the sweetest odour, when the crew had now given up hope in their severe sickness. They were at once freely relieved, and the sun shone forth; so they made out their land-marks and reached Naukratis. Then Herostratus, rushing from the ship with the image, and also with the green myrtle boughs that had suddenly come forth, dedicated them in the temple of Aphrodite. And having sacrificed to the goddess, and dedicated the image to Aphrodite, he called his friends and relations to a banquet in the temple itself, and gave to each of them also a garland of myrtle, to which he thereupon gave the name Naukratite." Such is Polycharmus' story, which is quoted to prove that the garlands called Naukratite were made of myrtle. This question does not immediately concern us at present, but neither the miracle recorded nor the probably erroneous date need distract our attention from the tradition that the tale

embodies. Evidently the writer had heard that
"statuettes of Aphrodite, a span high, of
archaic style," had been brought from Cyprus
and dedicated in her temple at Naukratis. Now
this description exactly fits a large number of
the statuettes that were found in the temenos
of Aphrodite, and precisely similar statuettes
are very frequently discovered in Cyprus.
They seem, indeed, to have been originally the
products of Phœnician art, and especially of
that branch of Phœnician art which was
established in Cyprus.

But, although we may thus see the origin of the
type of statuette we have now before us, neither
the subject represented nor the style of the representation can be thus summarily dismissed.
For all who have studied the earliest stages of
Greek art know that whenever the Greeks borrowed a form, they always infused into it new
life and meaning. Brunn's famous analogy[1]
cannot be too often quoted; "from the Phœnicians the Greeks borrowed only the alphabet
of art, as they did also of letters; in both alike
they spoke from the first in their own language."
But the tradition preserved by Polycharmus is
of great interest, as indicating a fact that we
learn also from a study of the statuettes themselves;—the fact that even at Naukratis the
Greeks did not borrow, as a rule, directly from
the Egyptians, but that even there the influence
of Cyprus was of the highest importance. To
this question we must return after some more
detailed examination of the statuettes themselves.

As to subject also, a simple and comprehen-
sive statement is obviously impossible. It will
perhaps be best to begin by distinguishing three
types, the standing male type, the standing
female type, and the seated type. Each of these
will require a separate discussion, first of what
seem the representative specimens, whether
earlier or later in period, and afterwards of the
many variations to which each has given rise.

_____
[1] Die Kunst bei Homer.

(45) The standing male type is represented
by some specimens reproduced upon Pl. I. in
Naukratis I. Other similar statues were found
during the later excavations, and may be seen
in the plates of this volume (XV. 13).

The type is well known, especially in Cyprus
and Rhodes, where examples of it are found in
abundance. But the fact is perhaps hardly yet
clearly recognized, that from these primitive
figures up to the magnificent athletes of perfect
Greek art, we can trace an unbroken succession
of type. This type is known by many names;
the small figures now before us are variously
interpreted; the life-size statues of the archaic
period commonly go by the title of Apollo; in
the finest period they are generally regarded as
athletes; but it can hardly be disputed that the
last is produced from the first by the long
process of artistic evolution.

But we are anticipating. The statuettes we
are now concerned with show hardly any promise
of such a future. Yet even among them we
may perhaps distinguish various stages of development. Not that these stages represent of
necessity a chronological sequence; an earlier
type often survives side by side with a later one
which has been produced from it.

Sometimes these figures are draped, sometimes nude. In the former case they often
have hardly any indication of the forms of the
body; the lines of the drapery are sometimes
mere cuts at the place where any garment ends.
This is an arrangement often found in Cyprus
and Rhodes; a specimen that exemplifies it well
was left last year at Bulak (so too Pl. XIV. 1.).
But such figures can hardly be said to belong
to Greek art at all, though they show, perhaps,
the material, without form and void, which the
spirit of Greek art was afterwards to fill with
life. We may see the beginnings of this influence in two different classes of statuettes. In
the one the drapery is discarded, and thus we
have at once before us the type that afterwards
was developed into the whole series of Greek

Apollos and athletes (Pl. XIV. 13) : in the other, though the drapery is retained, the forms of the body are clearly felt and indicated. In Pl. XIV. 14 may be seen a figure which shows at least some signs of this tendency. In the position of these figures and the objects which they carry we may observe a great variety even at this early period. Sometimes we find a musician, with harp (XIV. 14) ; we may compare this with the primitive figures of flute players that have been found in abundance, made either of glazed ware (Pl. XVII. 4; cf. Nauk. I. Pl. II. 7) or of alabaster. Another common type is a hunter, who is represented as bearing his weapons and his quarry. This is clearly the meaning of the figure represented on Pl. XIII. 7; he holds in his hands his bow and his hunting knife, and over his shoulders are slung two hares and two young boars. On his thigh was once a dedication, now unfortunately illegible, which doubtless recorded his name (Καλλι. . .) and dedication to the goddess of himself and his spoils. It is perhaps doubtful whether we are to regard as similar in its intention such a figure as that represented in Pl. XIV. 10. Here the man, whose figure is very conventionally executed, without much feeling for nature, holds by its hind legs and tail a lion or leopard, which rests its fore-paws on his feet. A hunter may thus dedicate his spoil; but perhaps this figure may have a mythological significance (cf. also Nauk. I. Pl. I. 1).

(46) We must now pass on to the other main type, which is, as we might expect in this temenos, of most frequent occurrence. This is a draped female figure, holding some object in front of her breast with one hand, with the other supporting her drapery. Such is the normal arrangement ; of course many variations in detail are to be met with. These female statuettes bear the same relation to the female statues in elaborate drapery found on almost all early Greek sites, as the male figures bear to

the later 'Apollos ' and athletes. Of the other type, without drapery, no early example was found in the temenos of Aphrodite.

In no instance is there any marked advance on the primitive statuettes of this simply draped class. Above the waist there is hardly ever any clear indication of the drapery, except sometimes round the neck. Beneath the waist there is sometimes a division between an upper and lower garment, usually in a curved line ; often there are a number of vertical folds, either at equal distances all round the body, or drawn together into one broad fold, descending from the hand that supports it down the front. Examples may be seen in Pl. XIV. ; the last arrangement most clearly in 4. Hardly a sign is given in any case of the way in which the drapery has been put on; it is no more than a thickness of some material, enveloping and obscuring to some extent the forms of the body, but with no form or independent existence of its own. These figures from Naukratis cannot indeed be distinguished in any way from the similar ones frequently found in Cyprus. Any of them might well be the "statuette of Aphrodite, a span high, of archaic style," which, as we have seen, Herostratus brought over from Paphos. Whether they really are statuettes of Aphrodite is a question that admits of some discussion; but of this we must say more hereafter.

These figures in almost all cases hold some object in front of their breast with one hand. Sometimes it is a flower (XIV. 11 ; XV. 5); often an animal ; thus XIV. 12 holds a bird, XIV. 8 a small goat, XV. 1 (which was not, however, found by my own workmen in this temenos, but was brought me from another part of the town) holds a large goat with both hands in front of her body.

(47) Various other types will be observed upon our plates, some closely allied to those

we have just been describing, some widely
diverging from them. The most interesting of
them are perhaps the seated figures, which
again remind us, on a smaller scale, of certain
statues that have been found upon Greek soil.
One, XIV. 3, bears a strong resemblance to the
Branchidæ statues, " si parva licet componere
magnis." But this seated male figure can hardly
be the product of a different art from that to
which we must assign the female figure with
her child, XIV. 7. Here, however, the resemblance to the well-known Egyptian Isis and
Horus type is one that could not under any
circumstances be overlooked—least of all in the
case of a statuette found upon Egyptian soil.
But whether even here the influence of Egypt
is direct or not may be open to some doubt.
The Egyptian origin of the type is, however,
beyond dispute ; it is perhaps the most persis-
tent type known. Its similarity is throughout
obvious, from Isis to the Madonna of Christian
art ; and a valuable link in the series is offered
by this rough little statuette. More distinctly
Egyptian in style is the little kneeling figure,
XIV. 2 ; it is worked in low relief upon both
sides. Two or three animals are worth notic-
ing ; for instance, the limestone lion, XIV. 7,
and the aquatic bird, XIV. 1. This is of terra
cotta, painted with brown and purple, like an
archaic vase. It resembles very closely in
colouring the swans or geese which so
frequently occur upon those vases ; but in its
general proportions it certainly seems nearer
to a duck. Some statuettes also served the
purpose of vases ; XIV. 11 is merely an alabastron, shaped at the top to resemble a human
breast and head. Head-shaped vases, such as
that represented in XIV. 5, are well known in
Cyprus and elsewhere. But no sign of a
mouth or spout can be seen on this head,
though it is made in two parts so that the top
will lift off. The parts may, however, have
been originally intended to be fastened together
in some way.

(48) If we now turn from these details to
take a more general view of the statuettes that
have been discovered at Naukratis, there are
two questions which at once meet us. In the
first place, what is the meaning and intention
of all these statuettes, male and female,
dedicated in the temple of Aphrodite ? And
then, how far are they to be considered as the
products of Greek art, or as directly connected
with it, and what place do they occupy in the
great series of which we have already seen
them to form a part?

The first of these questions cannot yet find
a definite and conclusive answer. These
statuettes cannot be disconnected from those
found in the temples of Cyprus on the one hand,
on the other on many of the most important
sites in Greece, Branchidæ and Delos and
Athens. But one thing is clear. All these
male figures and " Apollos " and athletes, all
these female statuettes and early draped statues
of Delos and Athens and other sites, all these
seated figures that have been found in or near
various temples, must for the solution of this
problem be considered as a single series.
Various varieties and developments of meaning
or purpose may belong to various regions and
periods ; but these must not be regarded as
independent, but as deviations from their
common prototypes. So long as this great
fact is lost to sight, no explanation or theory
can be more than partial and inadequate.
Without attempting to solve a question which
has never yet found a complete and satisfactory
answer, we may note one or two pieces of
evidence that may guide us a little nearer to
its ultimate decision. First we may observe
that all these statuettes are dedicated to
Aphrodite, yet many of them are male ; one
is certainly a hunter and his spoils, and probably bore his name, just as one of the Branchidæ statues states that it represents its
dedicator. On the other hand, one of the
female statuettes was dedicated by a man

Polybermus (Pl. XXI. 794); and, if we trust the evidence quoted by Athenæus, "span-high statuettes of Aphrodite" were dedicated in early times. Thus we seem still as far from a conclusion as ever. Our evidence seems to show that statuettes were dedicated sometimes representing the dedicator, and denoting perhaps his devotion to the service of the divinity; sometimes representing the goddess herself. But we have as yet nothing whatever to guide us in any attempt to draw a broad distinction between the two classes; and where the dedicator and the divinity are both of the same sex, the confusion in their representation is not as yet unravelled.

As regards the style of the statuettes, it is clear at a glance that the influence of Cyprus is paramount; and thus literary tradition is confirmed by the testimony of excavation. But, as was to be expected at a colony on Egyptian soil, those Cypriote types which are derived from Egypt are the most readily adopted. It is hard to say whether we must allow that there was any direct influence exercised by Egyptian art upon the artists of Naukratis; but in any case it was modified by the hybrid Phœnician character of Cypriote work. It is instructive to observe how far the art of statuary lags behind the sister art of vase-painting; while there are many vases from Naukratis that for beauty of decorative effect have never been surpassed, no statuette has been found which shows more than a small advance upon the models from which it was derived. This fact is most interesting when we remember that it was from Egypt [3] that Rhœcus and Theodorus of Samos are said to have learnt the innovations which they introduced into the still primitive art of Greece; and that Naukratis was the only town of Egypt which was in their time open to Greeks. Whether they studied the Egypto-Cypriote style prevalent among the artists of the colony, or went straight to the technical perfection of Egyptian statuary, is a question which can only be answered by conjecture; but in any case we now possess a most interesting reminiscence of their sojourn. In the temenos of Aphrodite at Naukratis was discovered a vase which had been dedicated to the goddess by Rhœcus—in all probability no other than this very artist, then pursuing in Egypt the studies that were afterwards to influence the sculpture of Greece.

---

[3] cf. Mitchell, Hist. Anc. Sculp. p. 199.

CHAPTER VII.

TEMENOS OF HERA.

(49) THE temenos of Hera, and the accident that led to its discovery, have already been mentioned. Herodotus had spoken of the temenos dedicated by the Samians to their goddess Hera as if it were as important as that of the Milesian Apollo. The two are side by side in the city, and we might reasonably have hoped that each would yield an equal treasure. Indeed, when we remembered the friendship of Amasis with Polycrates of Samos, and the offerings that he made at the Heræum in that island, we might well have regarded the temenos of Hera as the most promising of all sites at Naukratis. But all such expectations, as has been related, proved deceptive, owing partly to the digging of the Arabs, partly perhaps to other causes which we cannot now even conjecture. But it is unprofitable to discuss hopes that were not fulfilled; all that can now be done is to give some account of the results that actually did proceed from a careful exploration of the site.

The walls of the temenos, which is of very considerable extent (see general plan, Pl. IV.), had been completely traced by Mr. Petrie in the previous season; but he had then no evidence to lead to the true identification of the enclosure which they surrounded. He had indeed conjectured that it might be the Palæstra, because an inscription,[1] found elsewhere, recorded the dedication of the Palæstra to Apollo. Hence it seemed probable that the large enclosure adjoining the temenos of Apollo might be the Palæstra; but Mr. Petrie himself

---

See Nauk. I. Pl. XXX. p. 63.

only regarded this as a conjecture, not of course to be insisted on in the face of definite evidence. Such evidence has now been found, in the vases bearing incised or painted inscriptions of dedication to Hera; and accordingly the name of this great enclosure has been altered in the map.

In clearing the surface of the temenos, some traces of buildings were found. The most important of these presented an oblong plan, and its internal measurements were 56 feet from N. to S., 18 feet 10 inches from E. to W. It was surrounded by a low wall of mud brick, about twenty-six inches thick—much too thin to be the outer wall of a building of such dimensions. The whole space within this wall was carefully levelled, and had been covered with sand. Hence it seems clear that what is now left is only the foundation of an edifice once built of stone, surrounded, as in other cases at Naukratis, by a retaining wall of mud brick. The levelled surface is at a level of about 300 inches above the datum : thus this building ranks among the earliest at Naukratis. Was it the temple of Hera ? This is a question which cannot now be answered decisively; but its position and dimensions make such an identification extremely probable. The chief objection is that its narrower ends face north and south, not east and west, as is usual in the case of temples. But this is not a fatal objection; instances of such a situation are well known, as, for instance, in the case of the temple at Bassæ. But, on the other hand, there are here no exigencies of the ground to necessitate any such arrangement. On the whole, however, we seem hardly justified in asserting that a building of such dimensions, situated in the temenos of Hera, cannot have been the temple of the goddess.

One other structure calls for mention, though its intention cannot now be discovered. This structure appears to be the lower part of two pillars, with a plaster floor between them ; the level of their foundation is about a foot above that of the building just described. They are in a line with its east wall, at a distance of about nine feet from its southern extremity. But whether they formed a part of another building, or are an independent construction of which we cannot now conjecture the use, must remain in uncertainty. This is but a meagre and unsatisfactory account to give of the architectural remains found *in situ* upon a temenos of which so much had been expected ; but it is all that can be stated without entering the realm of baseless conjectures. One other architectural relic may here be noted, a piece of egg-moulding in limestone, probably from the earliest temple of Hera ; but its forms are not remarkable enough to be worth detailed description.

(50) If we turn next to the enumeration of the various objects found upon this site, we shall not find in them any richness to compensate for the poverty of its architectural remains. The most important are some vases and fragments of vases with dedications to Hera incised upon them ; these will be found in their due place on Pl. XXII. The vases themselves are not, in most cases, of much interest. A favourite type, however, in this temenos is a small cup with one handle—a shape which we find indeed elsewhere, in the temenos of Aphrodite for example, but which in no other place is so common as it is here. These cups are sometimes made of rough red ware, sometimes with a slight glaze, of a yellow or brown colour ; they also bear sometimes the name HPH in large letters.

Other articles that were found in the loose refuse scattered over this temenos need not be described here, as they do not properly belong to the sanctuary of the Samian Hera, but had only found their way into it by accident. They may either have been thrown here from other sites in the neighbourhood, or from higher strata that in later times had occupied the same ground, and had been successively dug away by the Arabs. It is possible even that the inscription, Ἱερὸν Διὸς Ἀποτροπαίου, to which we have already referred as giving the first clue that led to the identification of the site, may also have come here in this way. In any case its presence was fortunate, since it led to the identification of a temenos which is rich in associations though poor in remains, and which, if still unknown, might have led to a deceptive estimate of the treasures still buried at Naukratis.

CHAPTER VIII.

INSCRIPTIONS.

(51) It will be as well to state at once that the inscriptions found in 1885-6 are not, in importance and antiquity, comparable to those produced by the previous season's excavations: and that they do not throw any light upon the questions that have given rise to some controversy. That controversy cannot be ignored or passed over; but since no new facts are forthcoming which bear directly upon it, to deal with it here would only complicate its issues, and confuse the discussion of the new matter now before us. In the final chapter a few words will have to be said as to the details of the epigraphic evidence, and as to the light they throw on the age of the Greek colony at Naukratis. But at present we are only concerned with the interpretation and the transcription of the inscriptions found in the course of the last season. Here again the temenos of Aphrodite has yielded by far the most interesting and numerous collection. The circumstances of their discovery and the pottery on which they are incised have already been described. The inscriptions themselves will be found upon the large folding plate (Pl. XXI.).[1] They are mostly in the Ionic alphabet; the only exception that calls for special notice is that of the inscriptions 86-93, which are, as we shall see, in all probability Lesbian. If so, they are of great interest, and are by far the most important epigraphical discovery of the year at Naukratis: for hitherto no Lesbian inscription has been known previous to the general adoption of the Ionic alphabet. Hence both the letters and the dialect are important. But all such matters can best be discussed in immediate connection with the inscriptions to which they refer; I will therefore proceed at once to the transcription of these, adding such notes as may seem necessary or desirable in each case. I do not think I have omitted any inscriptions that are of interest either from their substance or the forms of their letters. Mere repetitions of ἀνέθηκεν and τῇ Ἀφροδίτῃ were obviously not worth recording.'

INSCRIPTIONS FROM THE TEMENOS OF APHRODITE.

Ornate bowls, painted both inside and out with animals in red on a white ground. (Pl. VI.) 701-705.

701.[2] Σώστρατός μ' ἀνέθηκεν τῆφροδίτη.

The inscription is also visible on Pl. VI. We find that between the article and noun hiatus, crasis, and prodelision are all allowed; here the second is found (ΤΗΦ); we might equally well have τῇ Ἀφροδίτη (ΤΗΙΑΦ), or τῇ 'φροδίτη (ΤΗΙΦ). I shall not again notice these varieties when they occur.

702-5. These may all be parts of a dedication precisely similar to 701; they are all from different fragments of the same bowl, of which only a few scattered pieces were found. 705 is on the outer rim, the rest inside. 702 has much older forms than 701; but the bowl was similar, and the name of the dedicator seems to have been the same in both cases. But we cannot

---

[1] The inscriptions have, with a few exceptions mentioned, been traced directly from the originals, and then copied by a photographic process. The forms of the letters may therefore be relied on as accurate.

[2] I begin with this number in order that these inscriptions may be consecutive with the series in Nauk. I., numbered 1-700.

believe that the same man dedicated both at the same period. The complete bowl, which is more careful and ornate in its style, may have been a later offering from the same man, to supersede his earlier gift.

White-glazed Naukratite ware; inscriptions incised on the body of the vase. 706-738.

706. . . . ης ὁ Χῖος. The Chians were among those who shared the privileges granted by Amasis to Naukratis. Her. ii. 178 ; cf. 757.

707. . . . ιθε(σ)τος ἀνέθηκ[ε τ]ῇ 'Αφροδ[ίτ]η[ι

708. . . . (μ)αιος ἀνέθηκε

709. . . . ος μ'ἀνέθηκε τῇ[ι 'Αφροδίτῃ] ἐπὶ τῇ. . . .

710. ὁ δεῖνα ἀνέθη]κε τῇ 'Αφροδίτῃ

711. Part of a name ?

712. 'Ι]υνξ ἀ[νέθηκε. As that of a daughter of Peitho (see Pape) this name may have been assumed by a Naukratito hetæra.

713, 714. Parts of names ?

715. Σ[. . . δ]νέθηκεν τῇ 'Αφροδίτῃ. On the bottom of a lamp of the central tube pattern, of white Naukratite ware.

716. 'Ερμό[τιμος ἀνέ]θηκε [τῇ 'Αφρ]οδίτ[η. This bustrophedon inscription is incised in the body of an ibex painted on this ware; it thus makes a pattern like the natural spots of the beast's skin.

717. ΚαῖϘος μ'[ἀνέ]θηκεν. Ϙ is here used, before ο ; the Η may be a mere mistake, but we find a peculiar use of this letter at Naxos (I.G.A. 407) and elsewhere.

718, 719. Parts of names ?

720. . . . ορος μ'ἀν[έθηκεν

721. Part of name ?

722. Μυσός μ'ἀνέθηκεν 'Ονομακρίτου [τῇ 'Αφρο]δίτ[η

723. "Ασος μ'ἀνέθηκεν. This name is only known as that of a town in Crete.

724, 725. Part of name ?

726. Καλλ⌐
Θαλ⌐ίαρχος ἀνέθηκεν

727. Part of name ?

728. Τύχων ἀνέθηκεν

729. "Αρχαιος ἀ[νέ]θηκεν τῇ' 'Αφροδίτῃ. "Αρχαιος as a name is new. The ι of the article here seems to be merely elided; if so, we have a fourth variety, beside the three mentioned on 701.

730. Part of name.

731. . . . λέω[ν ἀνέθηκεν

732. Πρωτογέ[νη]ς [ἀνέθηκεν

733. 'Ανέθηκεν. This and 738 are given, to show side by side the older and the later form of θ.

734. . . . ναξ μ'[ἀνέθηκεν

735. . . . πρῶτον . . . ?

736. . . . ων με ἀν[έθηκεν

737. 'Αράβα[ρχος or 'Αραβα[ιγύπτιος ?

738. See 735.

738*. In any case confused, the consonants being omitted. Perhaps the writer meant μ'ἀνέθηκεν 'Αφροδίτῃ.

White-glazed Naukratite ware, inscriptions painted in brown. 739-747.

739. 'Αφοδίτη (sic) ; the omission of the ρ is a common error, proceeding doubtless from its similarity to half of φ.

740. 'Αφροδίτη]ι Θήσαν[δρος. The name is new, but not impossible; or we may restore Διοπε]ίθης ἀν[έθηκεν.

741. Αἰγύπτι[ος. This is interesting, if indicating the nationality of the dedicator; cf. the second suggestion for 737. There is no authority for restoring 'Αφροδίτη] Αἰγυπτί[ᾳ ; the epithet is, however, applied to Zeus and Dionysus, but only late. See Pape.

742. . . . ηλος μ' ἀνέθηκεν.

743. Ζψίλος or Ζωίλος; the reading can hardly be doubtful, but the spelling is peculiar : cf. Τηἴος or Τήιος, Nauk. I. Pl. XXXV. No. 700 ; the first ι must represent a kind of y sound preceding the vowel.

744. 'Ο δεῖνα ἔ]δωκε. Such a form of dedication is here unusual ; but it seems the simplest restoration.

745. Μικὶς ἀνέθηκεν. This feminine name will bear the same relation to Μίκων and Μικίων as, e.g., Παρμενὶς to Παρμένων and Παρμενίων.

746. ... ιπις ά[νέθηκεν

747. Γα]ληνίω[ν or Γ]ληνίω[ν

Naukratite vases ; inscriptions incised on bottom.
748-761.

748-753 (except 751) are copied, not traced, since the curvature of the bases made it almost impossible to employ the latter process with satisfactory results.

748. 'Ερμησιφάνης μ'ἀνέθηκεν τήφροδίτη. This coils right round the base; a double stroke is placed between ν and ε, where the second line comes beneath the first.

749. Τήφροδίτη Φορτύλος ἀνέ[θηκεν.

750. Τῇ 'Αφροδί]τῃ 'Ερμαγαθῖνος μ'ἀνέθ[ηκεν ; in the second α the third stroke is probably a mere accident. The first part of a similar name may be seen in 762.

751. Δέρκης [ἀνέθηκ]εν τῇ 'Α[φροδίτῃ ; cf. Δερκύλος, &c.

752. Τῆς 'Αφ[ρ]οδίτη[ς ἀνέθη]κεν 'Ερμογένης. The first ς is turned backwards, as sometimes happens in early periods, while the direction of writing is still undecided. The Γ here approaches very near to the Ι form which we know at Corinth, and shows clearly how that form arose.

753. Εὐκλῆς ἀνέθηκεν ἱερὴν τήφροδίτη. The inscription is continuous round the base, the two asterisks coinciding. The closed η is in one case quite clear : beside the later forms of the same letter and of θ this is very remarkable, and shows how little reliance can be placed on a single form of one letter, apart from other evidence of date. But the form is normal and well known ; it preserves historical characteristics ; and so its appearance here in no way weakens the evidence of other abnormal forms.

754. Ψευδε. ... ὁ ... ου ἀνέθ[ηκεν. Ψεν ... is very common in Ægypto-Greek names ;

it means *the son of*, usually before the name of a deity.

755. Πολ]ύκαρ[πος ἀ]νέθη[κεν.

756. Probably a mistake for τῇ]ι 'Αφροδ[ίτῃ.

757. ... ὁ Χῖος. cf. 706.

758. ... Τ]εισα[μένου υἱός. ...] κλῆς [ἀνέθηκεν τῇ 'Αφροδίτη]ι ὁ Τ[ήιος

759. ? ἔ]κ στρα[τείας ἀνέθηκ]εν ?

760. ὁ δεῖνα ἀνέθηκε]ν ὁ Πει[. ...φαιδ](ρ)υντής? The last word is no more than a guess. It is known as the title of the officers who had charge of the statue at Olympia, and may have previously been used for temple servants elsewhere.

761. 'Η δεῖνα] Πυλία ἀπὸ ['Α. ... τῇ 'Αφροδίτη

Various rough ware ; inscriptions incised.
762-765.

762. 'Ερμαγαθ[ῖνος. This is on a cup like those often dedicated to Hera at Naukratis ; for the name, cf. 750.

763. ... τιάδης. On a jug, rough black glaze.

764. On the handle of a large light yellow amphora, of early type.

765. 'Αφρο[δίτη. On a piece of rough red ware.

Cyrenaic vases ; inscriptions incised. 766, 767.

766. 'Αφροδίτη Νεγόμανδρος [ἀνέθηκεν. The name Negomandrus has a Græco-Egyptian look.

767. 'Ο δεῖνα ἀνέθηκεν 'Αφροδ]ίτη ὁ Φ[ιλά]μμ[ωνος? The name seems probable for a Cyrenean.

Large bowls, descended from eye-bowl type. Friezes of animals outside, inside black or red glaze with circles of white and red. 768-770.

768. ... $\begin{cases} ου \\ οχ \\ οψ \end{cases}$ .... 'Αφροδί]τη τῇ ἐ(ν) Ναυκράτι. This is painted in white letters on the red glaze inside the bowl. It is of the utmost importance, since it proves beyond a doubt

that the pottery of this class was made at Naukratis.

769. Here again we see a closed η ; but 750 is a warning against using it as evidence of date. This and the next are incised.

770. . . . μης με ἀν[έθηκε τ]ἠφροδίτη[ι

Flat plates with edges raised, usually painted with animals inside; inscriptions incised, except 774. 771-777.

771. Χάρμ[η]ς με [ἀνέθηκεν

772. This and 773 are on a similar light-coloured ware, and may be parts of the same plate. Thus we may read : Ἐρμοκράτ[ης ἀνέθ]ηκε τῆφροδίτ[η. The writer seems to have made a false start with the first two letters.

774. These letters are painted in light red on the bottom of a plate.

775. Κ]λεόδημός με ἀ[νέ]θηκε τῆ Ἀ[φροδίτη.

776. Χάρμ[ης με ἀνέθηκ]ε τῆ[ι Ἀφροδίτη εὖ]χωλήν : εὐχωλὴ is especially used for an offering made in fulfilment of a vow. So frequently in Homer; cf. Herod. ii. 63, εὐχωλὰς ἐπιτελέοντες. Cf. also C.I.A. 397, &c.

777. Χά]ρμης με ἀνέθηκε τῆφροδίτη εὐχωλήν.

Χάρμης seems to have dedicated three similar plates—unless, indeed, some of the pieces belong to the same ; they are much broken.

Eye-bowl, of more elaborate design than usual ; see Plate VII. 1.

778. Ῥοῖℚος μ'ἀνέθηκε τ[ῆ Ἀφρ]οδίτη. Probably the famous early sculptor, Rhœcus ; see chap. vi. § 46.

Large bowls, narrowing towards the top, and with a flat rim, on which the inscription is often incised ; sometimes it is incised on the body of the bowl, just below. 779-785.

779. Ὁ δεῖνα ὁ. . . .] χιδέω [ἀνέθηκεν τῆ Ἀ]φροδίτη ὁ Τή[ιος.

780. Φίλις μ'ἀνέθηκε οὐπικά[ρτ]ους τῆ[ι Ἀφροδί[τη. The surface is much worn. Ἐπικάρτης seems a possible variation on Ἐπικράτης.

Apparently τῆ is written twice. The writer made the common slip of omitting the ρ of Ἀφροδίτη, and corrected it after writing the o. For the bowl on which this is inscribed, see Pl. X.

781. Θούτιμός με ἀνέθηκ[εν

782. Λεωδάμας.

783. Τελοφάνης? I know no other compound name beginning Τελο-. It is difficult to suggest a more satisfactory restoration.

784. Ἐρμοφάνης ἀνέθ[ηκεν] ὁ Ναυσιτέ[λους.

785. Ὁ δεῖνα] μ'ἀν[έθηκε τῆ Ἀφρ]οδίτη. Written from right to left.

A very peculiar ware, black throughout, and very highly polished on the surface ; decorated tripods, &c., large conical bases, and bowls with a flat rim are the most usual forms ; inscriptions incised. 786-793 ; cf. also 840.

786. Ὁ δεῖνα ὁ Μ]αλόεις Ἰο. . . . See after 793. Maloeis is an epithet, perhaps local, of Apollo in Lesbos ; may it be also used of one who lived by his sanctuary at the place named after him?

787. Τᾷ Ἀφροδίτᾳ

788. Ὁ δεῖνα κάθ]θηκε τᾷ Ἀφροδίτᾳ ὁ Μυτιλήναιος

789. Ὁ δεῖνά] {(με κά)}θηκε ὁ [Μυτιληναιος {(μ'ἀνέ)}

790. Ὁ δεῖνά μ]ε κάθθη[κε] ὁ Μυτ[ιλήναιος

791. Ὁ δεῖνα κ]άθθη[κε

792. . . . λη ἐμ[ε κάθθηκε

793. . . . . ων ἐ. . . .?

In this series of 8 inscriptions, distinguished from all the rest by the ware they are incised upon, we notice at once some striking peculiarities. Two are almost certainly dedicated by Mytilenæans; a third, 786, by a man of Μαλόεις,[1] a harbour in Lesbos with a temple of Apollo Maloeis, as we learn from Thucydides. All the inscriptions seem to be in the same alphabet and dialect ; a dialect which in every

---

[1] The first letter of this word is hardly doubtful ; it must be either μ or λ, from the traces left.

I

way corresponds to what we know of the Æolic of Lesbos. Twice also a peculiar formula of dedication, κάθθηκε, is found. Putting all these facts together, we may without rashness conclude that we have here specimens of the Lesbian dialect and alphabet. These are of the greatest importance, as no inscriptions were before known from that island of a date prior to the prevalence of the Ionic alphabet. We may now thus record the Lesbian alphabet ; it seems to have no peculiar forms.

A .. Δ Ē Ę .. ⊕ I K ʌ M ʌ/ .O . P ⋝ T . Φ Φ

As regards dialect, the most important fact to notice is that a double aspirate is used wherever possible ; thus we should probably write in Sappho's poems Σαφφώ (or Ψαφφώ), καχχέεται, &c. For these inscriptions are, perhaps, within 50 years of the date of Sappho's writing, and so supply by far the most trustworthy evidence now to be found as to her orthography. It is very remarkable that no Ϝ appears ; we should certainly have expected one in Μαλόεις ; cf. Maleventum.

Stone ; inscriptions incised. 794, 795.

79ɫ is on the back of a limestone statuette, representing a female figure. Πολύερμος μ'ἀν[έθηκε] τῇ 'Αφροδίτῃ.

795 is on the edge of a limestone dish, found just outside the temenos on the west ; the third line is inside the dish.

Εἴ]ς Να[ύ]κρατιν [ἀφικόμεν]ος ['Αφροδίτη]ι Καὶ Ϙο[ς ἀνέθηκεν. This is of great importance, from the scarcity of inscriptions that mention the name of the town.

Black and red bowls, mostly plain ; inscriptions incised. 796-826.

796. 'Ανέ]θηκ[εν
797. Τῆφροδί[τη
798. Δωρὶς φίλτ[ρον (?) 'Αφροδίτη.
799. 'Ωχίλος (?) μ'ἀνέθηκε. It is doubtful whether the name is complete or not ; in any case it is curious.

800. . . . βράτων με κ[άθηκε. This is not Ionic, if rightly read ; it resembles the Mytilensæan we recently met with.

801. 'Ελε] [σίβιος.
'Ηγη)

802. 'Αφρο]δίτῃι. Again non-Iouic.

803. Part of a name ?

804. 'Ηραγόρε[υς] | τῆφρο[διτ] | η ό. . . This was found near the top of the excavations, and probably does not belong to the remains of the first temple ; but it can hardly, from the forms of the letters, be later than the fifth century, B.C. If so, it is interesting, as showing, perhaps, the earliest known example of true ligatures. (Those of Amorgos are, at least, doubtful, and even if the connecting lines be part of the inscription as intended, they do not produce true ligatures, since the letters combined do not become integral parts of one another.)

805. Τεισά[μενος
806. 'Ισ]τίαιος ά[νέθηκεν . . .?
807. 'Αφροδί]τῃ ό Μ. . . . Non-Ionic.
808. Φυ]λλὶς ἀν[έθηκεν.
809. Part of a name ?
810. . . . ἄπα ά[νέθηκεν.
811. Part of a name ?
812. 'Αφροδίτ[η
813. . . . πος Διο. . . .
814. 'Αφροδ]ίτῃ ό Κε[. . . .—not ό Κεῖος ; the dialect precludes such a restoration.
814*. . . . όνης τ[ῇ 'Αφροδίτη
815. Μεγακλῆς
816. Τρωΐλος
817. 'Ο δεῖνα] καὶ Χ[ρυσ]όδωρός με ἀνέθ[ηκαν.
818. Πανδήμῳ ; sc. 'Αφροδίτῃ. This dedication is arranged on a fragment in such a way that it appears to have been incised after the vase was broken. Perhaps the sherd was used as a label for some articles that would not themselves bear an inscription.
819. Δ]άκρι[το]ς μ' | ἀνέ[θη]κε | ούρμο-[θ]έμ | [ιος] τῆφροδί | [τη
820. 'Ο δεῖνα ἀνέθηκε]ν τῇ 'Αφροδίτη.
821. Π]ανδήμῳ ; cf. 818.

822. Τλης ὁ Μυλήρου Ἀφροδίτῃ. On a black and buff bowl left at Bulak, ornamented inside with concentric circles.

823. Φοῖνιξ

824. Part of a name?

825. Ἀνέ]θηκε Ζωίλος Ὠι. . . .

826. Ὀηναθα? Incised on a vase with male and female dancing figures; in small letters, from r. to l. It may have some connection with the scene.

Black and red; inscriptions painted. All probably Attic, of second half of 6th century, B.C.
827-832.

827. . . . ας ἔγραψεν.

828. Ἐ]ργότιμος ἐ[ποίησεν

829. . . . ίας ἐ[ποίησεν

It is tempting to join these two, 828 and 829, together, and refer them to Klitias and Ergotimus, the famous artists of the François vase.

830, 831. . . . ἐποίησεν

832. . . . ἀνέθηκα

(52.) INSCRIPTIONS FROM THE TEMENOS OF THE DIOSCURI.

These do not, for the most part, call for much attention; they are of use to confirm the identification of the site on which they were discovered. See also Nauk. I. 665-682.

Black and red ware; inscriptions incised.
833-839.

833-836. Διοσϙ ούροις

837 and 839. Διοσκούροις

838. Ἀ]λεξιδήμο[ς ἀνέθηκεν. For the name, cf. Nauk. 1. 667.

Black ware, similar to that on which 786-793 are incised.

840. Νέαρχός με κα[τέθηκε το]ῖς Δ[ιοσκούροις. It is curious to find the formula κατέθηκε recurring on this black ware; but the dialect here seems not to be the Lesbian Æolic, which does not drop the final ι of the dative plural, τοῖς being accusative. There are hardly grounds

for attempting such a restoration as would bring this inscription into harmony with that dialect.

(53.) INSCRIPTIONS FROM THE TEMENOS OF HERA.

These again are only of interest as identifying the site.

Black and red ware; inscriptions incised.
841-845.

841-844. Ἥρη

845. Ἥρῃ

Cup; inscription incised.

846. Ἥρῃ. If this be the true reading, the inscription is from right to left, and the ρ is inversed. But the first stroke may be accidental, and if so we should read Ἥρη.

Cups; inscription painted.

847. Ἥρη

848. Ἥρῃ (?)

(54.) INSCRIPTIONS FROM OTHER SITES, INCISED ON POTTERY.

Painted on black and red ware (Attic).
849-852.

849, 850. Σόνδρος ἐποίησεν.

852. ἐποίησεν.

853, 854. The first painted, the other incised, on the same bowl.

853. Χαῖρε κα[ὶ πίει.

854. Ὕβλης.

855. Φιλ]οξένης Δ[ιοσκούροις

856. . . . ος Ἀπ[όλλωνι

857. . . . ων Ἥρῃ

860. Στράτω[ν

861. Σιμία. Late.

862. Ἑρμία[ι]ος ? Late.

862-874. On the bottoms of various vases, mostly black and red.

863. Ἀμεινο[κλῆς

864. A Cypriote character like this need not cause any surprise at Naukratis.

865-868. These numerals may have indicated measures, but more likely the number of vases in the lot to which they belonged; they denote 50, 10, 6, 10.

874. . . . ι Συρακόσιος. This is on a late vase, with a ribbed surface, and stamped ornaments inside. Hence it can hardly be earlier than Ptolemaic times; thus it indicates that punctuation such as that used here is not necessarily a proof of early date.

875. Φιλίππου. This is the owner's name, incised on the body of a large jug; the characters are not earlier than Ptolemaic.

On Pl. XX. will be found the following inscriptions, found in the season 1884-5, and left at Bulak. They are from Mr. Petrie's copies.

876. On the shoulder of a vase, with the pattern given below it. Ἑρμαγόρης μ'ἀνέθηκε ὁ Τ[ήιος] τὠπόλλωνι

877. Πύρ(ρ)ος με ἀνέθηκε. On the rim of a black and red bowl.

878. Τὠπόλλωνός [εἰμι. On a bowl with birds.

879. Ἀπόλλωνός εἰμι. On a bowl with birds.

880. Ἀπολλω. . . . In a red band of a black and red bowl.

881. Ἀπόλλωνός εἰμι. On a scarlet and red (?) eye-bowl. The second λ has been at first omitted, and afterwards inserted.

882. On Pl. xvii. 3, will be found a curious caricature, scratched on the bottom of a vase; round it runs the inscription Ἀπελλαμονείον and ΓΙΘΑΚΟ ΜΙΜΗΜΑΕ πιθάκου μίμημ' Ἑ. . . . Thus the satyr-like head, the "image of an ape," is doubtless described as the likeness of some one whom we may suppose to be Apellamon.

(55.) INSCRIPTIONS FROM VARIOUS SITES; ON STONE.

12 and 13.[1] Two sides of one thin marble tablet. The first is much earlier than the second, and it seems that the tablet may have been reversed and used a second time in the

---

[1] This numbering, as well as that of the inscriptions on pottery, continues that of Nauk. I.

fifth century, B.C., the older inscription being no longer wanted. The inscription was found about 100 yards east of the temenos of Aphrodite; but a search in the neighbourhood revealed no further indications of a sacred enclosure.

13. . . . ος | . . . . δεκά[την; the first letter of the second line must be λ, μ, or α; probably the last; if so, we may read ἀνέθηκα.

14. Ἱερὸν Δι[ὸς | ἀποτροπ[αίου. This has already been referred to as being found in the temenos of Hera.

15. . . . Ἀ]μμωνίου. . . . ἐν σ]υνόδῳ Σαμβαθικῇ (?). . . . . Καίσαρος φαμενώθ ζ'.

16. . . . πολυμόρφ[ῳ. -είαν ἐδώλην

Apparently from the basis of a statue, perhaps of Artemis Hecate, whom the epithet fits.

18. Πτολ]εμιαον | Φιλοπάτ]ορα Φι[λάδελφον. Ptolemy X., Auletes, or Neos Dionysus, used these two titles together.

19. Spes in Deo. A plaster Amphora stopping, of Christian period.

It will be convenient to notice here one or two inscriptions found at Naukratis previously, and as yet either unpublished, or not included in what has already been published as the product of Naukratis; these I will number in accordance with the plan already adopted.

20. Unpublished; from a copy made by Mr. F. Ll. Griffith.

ΕΝΘΑΔΕΔΝΜΕΛΙ . . . . ΧΕΙΧΘΩΝΠΟΥΛΥΒΟ-
ΤΕΙΡΑ
ΤΗΙΟΝΟΣ ΠΑΣΗΣ ΕΥΣΕΒΙΑΣ . ΕΤΟΧΩΣ
ΙΔΕΑΡΕΤΗ ΣΚΛΕΟΣΕΣΘ ΔΟΝΑΕΙΜΝΗΣΤΟ-
ΝΛΕΤΟΔΕΑΥΤΩΙ
ΜΝΗΜΕΙΟΝΦΑΝΕΡΟΝΤΟΙΣΕΠΙΓΙΝΟ-
ΜΕΝΟΙΣ
Ἐνθάδε δ(ὴ) Μελί[αν κατέ]χει χθὼν πουλυβό-
τειρα
Τήιον, ὃς πάσης εὐσεβίης [μ]έτοχ(ο)ς,
(ἠ)δὲ ἀρετῆς κλέος ἐσθ(λ)ὸν· ἀείμνηστον (δ)ὲ
τόδε αὐτῷ

μνημεῖον, φανερὸν τοῖς ἐπιγινομένοις. Or in the first line we may read Δ(η)μέ(a)[ν κατέ]χει; with an epigrammatic licence of scansion; thus the too short gap mentioned by Mr. Griffith will suffice.

Mr. Griffith adds the following note: "The inscription is badly cut in soft limestone, letters rather small. The Δ's seemed to be without the cross-line, but generally the top corner of the Δ was chipped out. A letter has been begun incorrectly after the first E of Εὐσεβίας. Four is the number I have put in my note-book as being lost between ΜΕΛΙ and ΧΕΙ, but the sense seems to require more." The inscription, so far as I can judge, seems to be of good period, neither very early nor very late; there are no data for any more exact statement; the third or second century B.C. is a not improbable period for it. The grammatical construction is possible, if we take ὅς. . . . μέτοχος as a parenthesis, and make ἐσθλὸν, in l. 3, agree with Μελίαν; or it is possible to take ἠδὲ ἀρετῆς closely with the line before, and make κλέος ἐσθλὸν in apposition to the sentence.

21. Published in the *Academy*, January 3, 1885, from a copy made by Mr. Griffith.

Νειλούσσης ἀλόχου τήνδ'εἰκόνα Παρθενοπαῖ[ου

μητρὸς δ'ἡμετέρας στήσαμεν ἐν τεμένει·
οὐ φθόνος ἀλλὰ ζῆλος ἐν ἀνδράσι γίνεται ἀνδρῶν
οἳ στῆσαν γονέων εἰκόνας ἀμφοτέρων·

It is not known in which temenos the statue of Neilussa was set up by her sons.

22. Mr. Augustus C. Merriam has published in the *American Journal of Archæology*, Vol. II. No. 2, an inscription in the collection of Mr. Joseph W. Drexel, obtained from Thebes. It runs as follows in Mr. Merriam's transcription :—

Ὑπὲρ β]ασιλέως Πτολεμαίου θε[οῦ
μ]εγάλου Φιλοπάτορος σωτῆρος
καὶ νικηφόρου, καὶ τοῦ υἱοῦ Πτολεμαίο[υ,
Ἴσιδι Σαράπιδι Ἀπόλλωνι
Κόμων Ἀσκληπιάδου
οἰκόνομος τῶν κατὰ Ναύκρατιν.

It is doubtful, as Mr. Merriam observes, whether Komon dedicated this tablet at Thebes or at Naukratis. It is no argument against the latter view that no trace was found in the excavations at Naukratis of an association of Apollo with Egyptian deities; for little or nothing was discovered in his temenos that came from Ptolemaic times. For further remarks on this inscription, see Mr. Merriam's paper.

CHAPTER IX.

CONCLUSION.

(56) THE date of the foundation of Naukratis, and the various historical problems associated therewith, have already been discussed by Mr. Petrie in Naukratis I. The discoveries that have been made since he wrote have not, for the most part, belonged to the earliest period of the city's growth, but rather to the time of its highest prosperity in the sixth century. It would not therefore have been necessary to re-open the discussion of its earliest history, but that the very existence of that earliest history has been called into question. Prof. Hirschfeld has published a paper in the *Rheinisches Museum*, xlii. p. 209 sq., the substance of which is, for our present purpose, summed up in these words ;

"Also frühestem ins Jahre 570, aber gewiss auch nicht viel später, d.h. nicht lange nach dem Beginn der Alleinherrschaft des Amasis, fällt der feste Punkt für all Arten von Denk-mälern, welche vom griechischen Naukratis erhalten sind." This is the conclusion Prof. Hirschfeld draws from the testimony of Hero-dotus. Earlier factories, such as the Μιλησίων τεῖχος mentioned by Strabo, may have existed before the time of Amasis, but these were not at Naukratis; they were, perhaps, absorbed into it on its foundation.

Such, in brief, is Prof. Hirschfeld's theory. I must refer to his paper (*loc. cit.*) those who wish to follow his arguments in detail, but I think the above will be found to be a fair state-ment of his position. Let us first examine the literary evidence on which the theory is, for the most part, based ; and afterwards consider

such evidence of excavation as tends to refute or confirm Prof. Hirschfeld's opinion. I may be excused if I here repeat some statements already made in Naukratis I. by Mr. Petrie. For the raising of this question has given to them a new bearing and importance.

Beyond vague traditions as to the foundation of Naukratis, mostly pointing to a Milesian origin, there are only two sufficiently circum-stantial to be of much use as evidence.

Strabo says (p. 801) : " τὸ Μιλησίων τεῖχος· πλεύσαντες γὰρ ἐπὶ Ψαμμητίχου τριάκοντα ναυσὶν Μιλήσιοι (κατὰ Κυαξάρη δ' οὗτος ἦν τὸν Μῆδον) κατέσχον εἰς τὸ Βολβίτινον · εἶτ' ἐκβάντες ἐτείχισαν τὸ λεχθὲν κτίσμα· χρόνῳ δ' ἀναπλεύ-σαντες εἰς τὸν Σαϊτικὸν νομὸν, καταναυμαχήσαντες Ἴναρον, πόλιν ἔκτισαν Ναύκρατιν οὐ πολὺ τῆς Σχεδίας ὕπερθεν." Here we are told that the Milesians first made a fortified post, the Μιλη-σίων τεῖχος : then " after a certain lapse of time they sailed up to the Saite nome, and having conquered Inarus in a naval fight, they founded the city of Naukratis, not far above Schedia." I do not agree with Mr. Petrie that " we cannot make use of this statement " because an Inarus lived in the fifth century. We need not assume the two to be identical : and the statement of Strabo is so clear and definite that he evidently is drawing from some well-informed author or tradition. If we find Herodotus and Strabo inconsistent, we may feel compelled to accept the statement of the former, as living nearer to the time he writes about. But we have no right to reject arbitrarily the story of Strabo, if it is confirmed by tradition, and shows no inconsistency with our other trustworthy authority.

The statement of Herodotus is of such importance that it must also be quoted in full; for various and opposite meanings have been extracted from it. "Φιλέλλην δὲ γενόμενος ὁ Ἄμασις ἄλλα τε ἐς Ἑλλήνων μετεξετέρους ἀπεδέξατο, καὶ δὴ καὶ τοῖσι ἀπικνευμένοισι ἐς Αἴγυπτον ἔδωκε Ναύκρατιν πόλιν ἐνοικῆσαι· τοῖσι δὲ μὴ βουλομένοισι αὐτῶν οἰκέειν, αὐτοῦ δὲ ναυτιλλομένοισι ἔδωκε χώρους ἐνιδρύσασθαι βωμοὺς καὶ τεμένεα θεοῖσι. τὸ μέν νυν μέγιστον αὐτῶν τέμενος καὶ οὐνομαστότατον ἐὸν καὶ χρησιμώτατον, καλεύμενον δὲ Ἑλλήνιον, αἴδε πόλιές εἰσι αἱ ἱδρυμέναι κοινῇ, Ἰώνων μὲν Χῖος καὶ Τέως καὶ Φώκαια καὶ Κλαζομεναί, Δωριέων δὲ Ῥόδος καὶ Κνίδος καὶ Ἁλικαρνησσὸς καὶ Φάσηλις, Αἰολέων δὲ ἡ Μυτιληναίων μούνη. τουτέων μέν ἐστι τοῦτο τὸ τέμενος, καὶ προστάτας τοῦ ἐμπορίου αὗται αἱ πόλιές εἰσι αἱ παρέχουσαι· ὅσαι δὲ ἄλλαι πόλιες μεταποιεῦνται, οὐδέν σφι μετεὸν μεταποιεῦνται. χωρὶς δὲ Αἰγινῆται ἐπ' ἑωυτῶν ἱδρύσαντο τέμενος Διός, καὶ ἄλλο Σάμιοι Ἥρης καὶ Μιλήσιοι Ἀπόλλωνος. ἦν δὲ τὸ παλαιὸν μούνη ἡ Ναύκρατις ἐμπόριον καὶ ἄλλο οὐδὲν Αἰγύπτου. κ.τ.λ."

I have quoted thus much in full, for fear of suppressing any words that may now or hereafter seem to have a bearing on the point at issue. What Herodotus actually asserts, then, is this; to those Greeks that came to Egypt, Amasis assigned the city of Naukratis to live in. Certain Greek states availed themselves of this privilege, founded a common sanctuary called the Hellenion, and enjoyed exclusive privileges. Separately from them, certain other Greek states, which had no share in these privileges, founded separate sanctuaries for themselves sacred to their national gods; thus the Milesians dedicated a temenos to Apollo.

From these words Mr. Petrie draws the very just inference "that the city of Naukratis existed before the time of Amasis." Prof.

Hirschfeld remarks, "After what Herodotus says, there cannot be any doubt that neither a Greek city nor Greek temples had been founded at the place before that king." I leave it to any unprejudiced reader to judge whether this inference can be drawn from the words I have just quoted. The statement of Herodotus might, I think, perfectly well describe the official assignment, or even the restriction of the Greeks to a site which some of them had already occupied for many years; it implies an enlargement and reorganization of the colony, but certainly does not imply that no Greek colony at all was there before.

So far I have referred only to the literary evidence; the testimony of excavation is far more decisive. Prof. Hirschfeld, arguing from Mr. Petrie's statement that the scarabs from the factory bear the names of the immediate predecessors of Amasis, but never of Amasis himself, writes as follows: "Wo Griechen einziehen mit ihren Göttern und Heiligthümern, wohnt fürder kein Aegypter: die Skarabaeen hören auf—die Reihe der griechischen Inschriften beginnt." In answer to this I cannot do better than quote Mr. Petrie's own words (Academy, July 16th, 1887). "The Greek foundation of Naukratis, long before Amasis, is so clearly shown by the remains found, that epigraphists would do well to pause and consider whether they have as good evidence from any other place to authenticate a different view. To take one point of the simplest kind: the scarab-factory in Naukratis was clearly in Greek hands, for the Greek export trade to Rhodes; the hieroglyphic inscriptions are continually blundered, and many of the designs are such as no Egyptian could have made. We are asked then . . . to believe that Greeks in a town supposed to have been founded by Amasis continually made scarabs bearing the names of his predecessors, but never commemorated the king who was most important in their view. If Amasis first settled the Greeks there, we should not expect to find the names of deceased kings of the previous line, whereas their names often occur; and we should expect to find his name, but it has never yet turned up. . . . But this scarab-factory is not the oldest thing in the town. Two feet beneath it—and two feet take half a century to accumulate, on an average—there is a burnt stratum which underlies all the south half of the town. Everything out of this stratum is distinctively Greek, and not Egyptian, and there is not a trace of Egyptian remains in the earlier parts in general." I may add that together with the scarabs in the scarab-factory were found buried numerous fragments of Greek pottery of various early styles.

Thus we have indisputable evidence that there were Greeks at Naukratis before the reign of Amasis, while Professor Hirschfeld's theory, that the settlement was Egyptian before that king, is entirely at variance with the testimony of facts. I have left out of the question for the present the epigraphic evidence: the proof is strong enough without it, and it can best be treated separately. All that remains for us now is to reconcile, if possible, the evidence of excavation with that of literature—not, I think, a very hard task.

Strabo[1] tells us (loc. cit.) that Milesians founded a fortified post in the reign of Psammetichus I., and subsequently moved up the Nile to Naukratis. Whether this took place during the same reign or later is not stated; but the testimony of excavation, as recorded by Mr. Petrie, points to the earlier origin. In any case, it must have been before the reign of Amasis; for after his reorganization the Milesians could not be spoken of as founding

Naukratis. The Milesians then, and possibly some other Greeks also, were at Naukratis before the accession of Amasis. When he officially founded and reorganized the colony, as is related by Herodotus, granting exclusive privileges to those Greek states that shared the Hellenion, the Milesians held aloof, perhaps from hostility to Amasis, perhaps from jealousy of the new colonists who invaded their old settlement. But they by themselves continued to live there, and to worship in their old sanctuary of the Milesian Apollo.

When Herodotus came, the new colonists had, by the help of their privileges, gained the upper hand; and so he did not recognize in the temenos of Apollo the original religious centre of the colony and its former occupants, but looked on it only as a separate foundation for a local cult. If this be the case, the statements both of Strabo and of Herodotus are quite as accurate as any one could expect; and there is no need to reject the one and to accept the other —a desperate course when the sum of our evidence is so scanty.

The only important point in which my theory differs from Mr. Petrie's is that I do not claim for the Hellenion an earlier date than the reign of Amasis, and he does not himself insist on any archæological evidence that it was earlier, beyond the mere historical probability.

(57) So far I have entirely ignored the evidence of inscriptions. I believe that evidence to be entirely in favour of the view I have just expressed; but it seems better, where it is possible, to establish my conclusion independently of the testimony of epigraphy; for the absence of very early inscriptions cannot be said to disprove the settlement of Greeks at Naukratis before the time of Amasis, though the presence of such inscriptions would prove it. We have now seen that there was a Greek colony, probably a Milesian colony, at Naukratis, founded some time before Amasis; perhaps about the middle of the seventh century B.C.

---

[1] Prof. Hirschfeld's ingenious and probable conjecture, that the poem of Apollonius Rhodius on the "Founding of Naukratis" was the basis of later tradition, in no way impairs the evidence of that tradition. For the Alexandrian poets were most painstaking about details of history and archæology.

It remains for us to consider whether we have sufficient grounds for attributing to the earliest years of the colony certain very curious inscriptions that were found by Mr. Petrie last year in the temenos of the Milesian Apollo. I assigned them last year (Nauk. I. chap vii.; cf. also *Jour. Hell. Stud.* 1886, p. 220, sqq.) to that period, and accordingly regarded them as the earliest representative specimens of the Ionic alphabet. Both Professor Kirchhoff, in the new edition of his studies, and Professor Hirschfeld[1] have contended that these inscriptions are no earlier than the rest that were found on the same site, and are all of them as late as the time of Amasis; they explain the various abnormal forms that occur as due only to the caprice, ignorance, or unskilfulness of the writers. The position taken by so high authorities necessitates a careful reconsideration of all the evidence that points to an earlier date. That evidence I will now recapitulate.

Let us first consider the first three classes of my table in Naukratis I. Pl. XXXV. A; that is to say, the inscriptions on Pl. XXXII. numbered 3, 4, 1b, 68-79 (omitting for the present 305). These include all the inscriptions incised upon three very early types of pottery : all were found low in the rubbish trench, except 3 and 4, which were at the bottom of an early well. Thus the testimony alike of excavation and of fabric points to their very high antiquity. That of epigraphy is as follows. On these vases we find incised inscriptions of an extremely primitive appearance. In the forms of some of the letters there is not much scope for variation; but the forms are primitive, except that of ι, which is straight ; but a straight line is a possible early abbreviation of the Phœnician yod. As to other letters in which deviation is possible, the following statistics will speak for themselves :—

	Normal Forms.	Doubtful.	Abnormal Forms.
ε	3		2
μ	1	1	2
ν	(1)[1]		2
σ	(1)[2]		4
	—	—	—
	5	1	10

If I add that the abnormal forms are, with the exception of one σ, identical in all cases, that the inscriptions are classed together from their style of pottery, not from the forms of their letters, and that the manners in which they are incised are quite different, and betray different hands, it will, I think, become clear that to attribute all the abnormal forms to individual caprice or ignorance is to assume a series of coincidences that would be truly incredible. We must, on such a hypothesis, believe that certain independent dedicators made certain identical mistakes, and no others ; that those dedicators happened all to select certain very early types of pottery, used by no one else, for their inscriptions; and that then these inscriptions all happened to get buried among the earliest fragments. But there is yet another point. None of these abnormal forms are by any means natural deviations from the ordinary Greek letters; they all can very easily be derived from the Phœnician characters, the recognized prototype of the Greek alphabet, or from other more or less direct influences that affected its earliest origin and forms. Thus our ignorant dedicators must have chanced upon yet another coincidence, and reproduced the very forms that their fathers must have used when gradually striving to write Greek in Phœnician characters. But surely enough has been said of these coincidences. The only possible inference from the facts just adduced is that the inscriptions before us are the earliest found at Naukratis, and that they date from the seventh century, when the alphabet

---

[1] Rh. Mus. *loc. cit.*

[2] These two forms are in the same inscription, which bears a late appearance.

was yet a new and unfamiliar adaptation from Phœnicia.

In the case of Class IV. our evidence is not quite so strong; for its vases are selected for the forms of their letters, not for their fabric, which is similar to that of many others found with them. But they serve rather to confirm than to weaken the evidence of the classes just discussed; the pottery is of a type that may very well be nearly as old as the others; and the peculiar inscriptions may also be the earliest—or at least preserve the tradition of the earliest forms. With them may be classed the peculiar inscription, 305; but there the resemblance of μ to the Phœnician may be due to a later and direct Phœnician influence—it may indeed have been incised by one who knew the Phœnician alphabet as well as the Greek. But an example like this cannot weaken the consistent testimony of the early inscriptions that we have just discussed; and I think their early date is at least as well proved on archœological and epigraphical evidence as that of any other set of inscriptions that is allowed a place among the primitive monuments of the Greek alphabet.

The last two sections have, I fear, assumed a somewhat controversial tone; but such a tone could hardly be avoided in discussing various views that affect the whole basis of our work at Naukratis. It is of course a great advantage to receive so careful a criticism before our work is completed; and my thanks are especially due to Prof. Hirschfeld for joining me in an elaborate discussion of our views in the *Academy*—a discussion that has done much to clear up the obscurities of the subject and to reveal the points at issue. If I am unable to finally agree to his conclusions, it is from no wish to ignore his arguments, or to underrate the ability with which they are put forth.

One more point must be noticed. If scholars should agree to accept Prof. Hirschfeld's most

ingenious distinction between the Rhodian and the Ionic inscriptions of Abu Simbel, it will indeed follow that the Ionic alphabet of Teos and Colophon is different from the Ionic alphabet of Naukratis. But there is still nothing to prevent the difference from being one of place, not of period. There are no reasons for assuming that all Ionian cities used precisely the same alphabet in early times; such a supposition is indeed contrary to the analogy of all other early alphabets, which invariably show strong local divergences, even if closely allied. And it is by no means impossible that the alphabet of the colony of Naukratis had adopted from Cyprus[4] Ω and the other 'complementary' characters at a time when they were unknown even to its parent city Miletus. But in that case Naukratis exhibits the earliest examples of that complete Greek alphabet commonly known by the name "Ionic," but certainly not common to all cities of Ionian origin. The unity of the early Ionic alphabet has never been proved, though it is commonly assumed: and if new facts are contrary to that assumption, it must be discarded.

(58) Let us now make a brief review of the actual results that have been gained by the second season's work at Naukratis. The present volume opened with some account of what had to be sought in the city, and of the fruits of the first season's excavation. To the sites already marked in Mr. Petrie's Plan of 1885 we may now add the temple of the Dioscuri, the temenos dedicated by the Samians to Hera, and the temple and temenos of Aphrodite. All these sites have been carefully cleared; and although the first two were somewhat disappointing, the third yielded a treasure of archaic vases, statuettes, and inscriptions, that surpassed even the anticipations aroused in the previous season. Thus of the sacred

---

[4] See Journ. Hell. Stud., 1886, p. 233.

sites we know from literary evidence the temenos dedicated by the Æginetans to Zeus alone remains buried. The cemetery of the ancient city has also been discovered, but the burials discovered certainly do not for the most part date from the richest and most prosperous period of its history. The greater and more important part of that cemetery may very likely be yet undiscovered, or may lie where it cannot without great difficulty and expense be excavated, beneath the modern Arab village on the mound to the north of the ancient site. Thus something still remains to be done; but during the following season, 1886-7, no work has taken place on the site, and it is, perhaps, improbable that any considerable results would reward an explorer who now resumed the excavations. In the course of time the Arabs will lay bare by their own digging those parts of the city that are still covered with the deep accumulation of centuries; and if then the site be revisited by some competent explorer, it may be possible to recover further vestiges of the ancient colony. There is, however, little reason to suppose that as much still lies buried as has already been brought to light: and this volume, together with its predecessor, must, for the present at least, be offered to those interested in the early relations of Greece and Egypt as representing the outlines of the knowledge that we have acquired from the excavation of the colony of Naukratis. Even if all our conclusions be not accepted, we may at least hope that our volumes and plates will serve as a storehouse of facts that throw light on the history of the Greeks in Egypt, and especially on the development of their manufacture and their art.

APPENDIX.

EGYPTOLOGICAL NOTES FROM NAUKRATIS AND THE NEIGHBOURHOOD.

By F. Ll. Griffith.

Kûm el Ḥiṣn, Ḥuṣn, or sometimes (in the mouths of Arabs) Ḥoṣn (كوم الحصن), is an important mound six and a half miles due south of Kûm Gaʿêf (Naukratis). It is more than a mile in circumference and nearly a third of a mile across from east to west. The mound has been deeply excavated by the *sebakhín*, who have skeletonized the northern portion of it, leaving only the house-walls standing. On the south-east side is a heap of sand and dust, which being less profitable than the house rubbish has been allowed to remain longer. Formerly it must have been below the level of the main part of the mound. Now, however, the latter has been cleared down to it, and in the last few years the heap of dust itself has been attacked. It was here, as I learnt from the *sebakhín*, that six or seven years ago the third known copy of the decree of Canopus in favour of Ptolemy Euergetes and Berenice was found (Cat. Bulak, 1883, no. 5401, p. 354). In the spring of 1884, when Mr. Petrie was visiting the ruins in this neighbourhood, he copied an inscription from a Ramesside monument that had been uncovered on the same spot (cf. Naukratis, vol. I., ch. xii.). In December, 1885, I visited the mound several times, and found that the heap of blown dust marked the site of a temple, the enclosure wall of which was partly visible. The only other remains were four monuments of Rameses II., in sandstone and granite.

A rough plan of the enclosure, with the position of the monuments marked upon it, is given in Pl. XXIV. The enclosure is apparently rectangular, measuring 127 yards east and west by 70 north and south. The walls, four yards thick, rest on rubbish piled to some height above water-level. The *sebakhín* have dug below the foundations and have almost entirely cut away large portions of the wall on the south, while the north side is much hidden by rubbish, but in no part is more than a few feet of the height remaining. The bricks are large, nine by eighteen inches. The foundation of the southern side of the pylon at the east end is distinct. It begins fifteen yards north of the south-east corner, and measures fifteen yards by ten. It is sunk deeper than the wall and is built of brick eight to nine inches wide. The north half of the pylon is hidden, but if this side of the enclosure was seventy yards long, like the west end, and the gateway was in the centre of the side, we may allow thirty yards for the wall and pylon foundations on the north and obtain ten yards as the breadth of the passage, not reckoning the stone facing of the pylon, which may have reduced the width.

Within this enclosure lie four monuments of Rameses II. The *sebakhín* told me that they had all been shifted since their first discovery, but they evidently still remain close to their original position. A sandstone group,

No. I.[1] on plan, represents the king seated with a goddess at his side. No. II.,[2] of quartzite, represents the same pair standing. Both of these have lost their upper parts. They now lie about thirty yards west of the pylon, and probably flanked the entrance to the temple itself. No. III. is a sandstone statue of Rameses, very much damaged; No. IV.[3] is apparently well preserved, in red granite. It lies partly on the remains of the pylon, and, like its companion, was almost hidden by rubbish. I could only uncover part of it. It represents Rameses standing, holding one, or perhaps two, inscribed staves or standards. III. and IV. may have stood just inside the gateway.

The inscriptions upon these monuments (see Pl. XXIV.) show that the mound is the site of Amu (or perhaps more correctly Àamu), 𓏤𓏤𓏤𓊖. Rameses is said to be "beloved of Sekhet, mistress of Amu;" "of Sekhet Hathor, mistress of Amu;" "of Hathor, mistress of Amu," and "of Sekhet, mistress of Iuiu;[4] "of Pa Rā, (the sun)," and "of Ptah neb maā.

Amu 𓏤𓏤𓏤𓊖 is frequently mentioned in papyri in connection with the worship of Hathor, and at Edfu it occurs under the form 𓊪𓂋𓏤𓏤𓏤𓊖, Pa neb amu, "residence of the mistress of Amu," as capital of the third nome of Lower Egypt,

---

[1] This measures across back, 40 in.; side of base, 36 in.; height of base, 15 in.; from foot to top, 24 in. Besides the inscriptions in the plate, the cartouches occur also on the upper part of the side of the throne, and on the front of the base.

[2] Hathor is on the left of the king. Base : side, 33in.; front, 42; height, 16. Cartouches on front of base and back support between the figures. In the latter place it is deeply sunk, suggesting an alteration.

[3] On the back are two similar parallel columns of inscription with the royal standard and names followed by the group IV.a. The right side is plain; on the left are two columns of names and titles with IV. b.

[4] Iuiu may be compared with Ibyc (cf. p.   ). Perhaps also with the name of the god Uu Khant Ament, "Uu Chief of the West," a form of Osiris whose festival was held at Auu, according to the list at Dendurah in Brugsch, Geog. iii., p. 15, and Taf. xii.

called 𓊖, ament or 'the west.' In this list it replaces 𓉐𓈖𓊖, Hat aht (house of the cow), of the other lists, which may, however, be identical with it.

Of Ptah, as connected with the city, I know nothing. In the nome lists and papyri Hathor appears as mistress of Amu. On these monuments, however, as well as on the tablet in Pl. XXIII., Sekhet appears to hold an equal or higher place. The difficulty is readily explained. According to a papyrus quoted by Brugsch in his geographical dictionary, Hathor is Uat' in the north, Sekhet in the west, Bast in the east. Still more important for us is the passage in the legend of the destruction of mankind by Rā, which brings Hathor, Sekhet and Rā (=Pa rā) into connection with the city. The eye of Rā was sent out in the form of Hathor to destroy the conspirators in the desert. She slew many, and, as Sekhet, trampled on their corpses for the space of several nights, beginning at Heracleopolis. Rā, who was in the great 'temple' of Heliopolis, repenting, sent in haste for mandrakes from Elephantine. When they were brought they were ground in the mill at Heliopolis, and mingled with human blood. The liquid filled 7000 jars. In the night the fields were inundated with it. The goddess drank to the full, and, becoming intoxicated, could not continue the slaughter. Rā then recalled her, using, according to one text,[5] the epithet 𓊪𓁐𓂝, àamit, 'gracious;' hence, add both the texts, is the origin of the maidens of Amu. Rā then ordained an annual feast at which jars of intoxicating liquor should be made according to the number of temple servants. This custom was henceforth observed by all men on the first day of the feast of Hathor (see Naville, Trans. S.B.A. viii., p. 413 ff., 1885).

---

[5] Sekhmit, 𓆙𓃒𓏤𓂝, the variant in this passage, meaning "powerful," evidently contains a play on the name of the goddess Sekhet or Sekhemt, 𓆙𓆓𓊖.

From these two passages we are prepared to find that the mistress of Amu was Hathor in her form of Sekhet, and we are not surprised to find them upon an equal footing, and that the two appear as one goddess, Sekhet-Hathor, on one of the monuments. The myth of Rā is found in the tombs of Seti I. and Rameses III. It was therefore especially prevalent under the XIXth and XXth dynasties, and it was natural that Rā should appear on these monuments even if otherwise he had no particular connection with the city. But probably the festival which he ordained to commemorate his act of mercy was celebrated at Amu, and in it Rā must have been as prominent as Sekhet-Hathor.

The interest of the site as the capital of the nome of Ameut, and the centre of the worship of Sekhet-Hathor, is considerable. Extensive excavations would probably not repay the Fund, but Kûm el Ḥiṣn is one of those numerous sites in the Delta where, while the lover of Egyptian archaeology grieves over the destruction of almost everything, he cannot but hope to save something of unique interest to science by the expenditure of a small amount of time and money on trials in the most likely places, which may after all lead to unexpectedly rich discoveries.

It must be remembered that as yet no pre-Ramesside monuments have been found in the west of the Delta, nor has any Egyptian site been excavated in that quarter.

I append a few notes upon some villages and sites in the neighbourhood. The names were taken down carefully from the mouths of native fellahîn, and sometimes from Arabs also. I omit the names of those hamlets which, being of quite modern origin, are called by the names of neighbouring villages, or of the wealthy proprietor who founded them, with the term 'Ezbe prefixed. The names can generally be recognized on the map of the Delta by Mahmud Bey, and the new map founded upon it and issued by the War Office. Both of these maps

are very complete, and fairly correct as to situations. The map of the French Expedition is, however, as far as it goes, unrivalled for accuracy and information as to the character of the country. The War Office and French maps are indicated by English and French respectively. Kûm el Ḥiṣn is not marked upon any of them.

1. Besûm, بسوم.
2. Ṭût (*sic*), الطود.
3. Biyûqa.
4. Ḥûme.
5. Abû-Samadheh.
6. Ramsîs.
7. Kûm Zemrân, كوم زمران.
8. Zemrân en naḥl, زمران النخل.
9. Ed delengât, الدلنجات (Fellâḥîn name) = Ṭaiyebet lism طبت لسم (Arab name).
10. Zauyet Mesallem.
11. Ihye (Abia el Hamra of the maps).
12. Kûm Efrîn or Ferîn, كوم فرين.
13. El ḥagar el maḥrûq, الحجر المحروق.
14. Rezzâfe, رزافه.
15. Nebîre (Fr., but on wrong side of canal. Eng., En-Nobaireh).
16. Ga'êf and Kûm Ga'êf, كوم جعيف.
17. Gebâris, جبارس.
18. Neqrâsh, النقراش.
19. Teh (el bârûd).

The first five lie within a mile of the mound. Ṭut lies between Besûm-eš-šerqyje and Biyûqa. Besûm-el-ġarbîye is continuous with Biyûqa on the south; east of it is a broad stretch of sand with pottery on the surface, which may prove to contain the cemetery of Amu. Khême is almost deserted. It lies a short distance west of 5. 6 is an insignificant village, on level ground. A bank at the north end, twenty yards long by five broad, though showing nothing but late red brick, has been more extensive, and may, on the strength of the name, mark the site of a small chateau of Rameses. There is an inscribed fragment in the mosque, with part of a Ptolemaic standard name. 7 stands on a small high mound, deeply excavated, but showing nothing early. In the northern mosque is a limestone slab with the name of Rameses II. I bought here the curious terra cotta figure no. 7 in Pl. XV. It is 7½ inches high, and plain at the back. The woman holds an object like a drum. Her head-dress, which is deeply ribbed, is evidently intended to imitate the Egyptian *nemmes*. It ends in two long tassels on the chest. It cannot, I think, be of true Egyptian work. 8. Nakhleh means "palm-tree," a remarkable coincidence if Amu means the "city of palm-trees." But it is curious, notwithstanding its proximity to the desert and the occasional out-crops of sand above the alluvium, that the district round Kûm el Ḥiṣn is not now at all remarkable for abundance of palm-trees. It is not clear from the remains whether the city flourished down to Roman times. Andropolis is placed by Ptolemy on the west of the Great River, between Letopolis (near the apex of the Delta) and Naukratis. If the form of the name had not been settled by its recurrence as Andro in the Antonine Itinerary it would have been tempting to read Δένδρων for Ἀνδρῶν, connecting it with the city of palm-trees (Amu), and finding a survival of the Greek name in Zemrân.

12. A large mound two and a half miles south-west of Sîdî Ómar (on English map), consisting of two large enclosures. The eastern enclosure (probably Saite, repaired in Ptolemaic and Roman times) with gates N.S.E.(?) and W., contained on the east the chief part of the town, now much excavated. In this is a small Saite temple enclosure (see Naukratis, Part I., ch. xii.). West of this was a large open space(?) through which a paved roadway ran from the temple to the west gate. The western enclosure, which is separated by a short space from the other, is apparently late, but square shouldered pottery whorls (different from the rounded Naukratis specimens) were picked up in the south-west corner. They are the only specimens in clay that I have seen in Egypt except those from Naukratis. I found a

channelled scarab mould in the early part of the town.

If Ibye, lying between Kûm el Ḥiṣn and Kûm Efrîn, may be taken as corresponding in name with Iuiu, 〈hieroglyphs〉 may, perhaps, be the ancient name of Kûm Efrîn, three miles north-west of Ibye. Kûm Efrîn, being on the edge of a broad strip of desert, would well account for the determinative in the hieroglyphic group, which seems to imply a border city or district inhabited by an alien race. Iuiu, therefore, may equally well be the name of a border district, small or large, which now survives as the denomination of only a single village.

15. On west bank of canal, opposite north end of Naukratis mound. It stands on a low mound. 16. At south end of mound of Naukratis, called by natives Kûm Ga'ef. This seems to correspond to "Telt Abqa" of the French map. 17. On a low mound. 18. Three quarters of a mile east of Kûm Ga'ef, on a low mound. It seems to preserve the name of Naukratis. Ναύκρατις=Neqrâsh is indeed against the analogy of Ναυπλία=Navplia or Navplion. The first syllable is shortened in Ναύπακτος = Epacto, but there the second syllable was long. We must suppose that the accent on the second syllable was sufficient in Egypt to shorten the first.[6] This is the only certain instance of a Greek local name kept up by the fellahîn.[7] A Greek inscription on a block of limestone, not yet published, lay amongst some farm buildings at Neqrâsh, but has been removed, and a fragment of granite with hieroglyphics lies at a corner of the houses by the side of the road.

---

[6] I had doubts about the length of the α, but Mr. Gardner, agreeing with the above explanation, has supplied me with the following authorities :—Ναυκρᾱτίτης, Callim. Ep. xl. Ναυκρᾶτις, Posid. apud Athen. xiii. p. 596 d, and there is no trace of a different value having been assigned. Ναύκρατις has authority as well as Ναυκράτις (gen. -ιος).

[7] Iskenderîyeh (Alexandria) being pure Arabic.

I have bought there several early antiquities, including a lotus-bud, broken from the breast of a
large statue in alabaster. They seem, however, to have come from Ga'ef. No early
remains were visible on the surface, and Mr.
Gardner's excavations have led to no result.
19. There are low mounds at Teh on both sides
of the railway, and Mr. Petrie adds, an enclosure with chips.

There are a few notes to be added to the
above chapter, which was written in the autumn
of 1886. First, as to the plate of the hieroglyphic inscriptions of Naukratis, which will be
recognized as the work of Mme. Naville :—

No. 1 is the inscription on the limestone figure
from some place in the neighbourhood (Naukratis I., § 115). It represents, 1 B, the prince
in the nome of Sap (meaning as often elsewhere, Sap meh or Sais) Psemthek-senb, son
of the divine father, Hori. His mother's name,
as we learn from the inscription on the back,
1 A, was Septith. 1 A also contains a common
funeral formula, a prayer to Tum ? for a good
old age in his home, with happiness, and burial
in his own tomb in the necropolis . . . a good
journey on the road to the west along which
the perfected travel.

In B he states "I was a man devoted to his [8]
[lord (the king or a god)], doing the right
according to his wish every day. I built his
house anew upon the east side ?[2] of the facade
of the temple of Neith after it had been over-
thrown."

1 c. "He . . . the buildings of the ancestors :
I enriched his tables : I performed the sacred
rites for his kas.[9] (This) I did in order that
the temples in Sais, the city of Neith, might
not be destroyed for ever."

Nothing more seems to be known of this
Psemthek-senb, which was a common name at or

after the XXVIth dynasty. The overthrow
(sekhen is a forcible word) of the temple or
palace might have taken place on the invasion
of Cambyses, or perhaps of Nebuchadnezzar.

Hori is a name known in Leiblein (no. 1230,
XXIInd dynasty).

2 is a small limestone tablet (see Naukratis
I., l.c.). It was brought to us at Nebireh on
market-day, apparently from a distance, and
although said to have been found at Ga'ef, must
have come from Kûm el Hisn or Kûm Efrîn.
Nebt Amu (Hathor) is perhaps to be distinguished from Sekhet, but more probably the
inscription is blundered here as well as in the
name of Amu. The prayer is to the goddess to
grant offerings from her (N.B. sing.) altar daily
to the ka of the scribe . . . Hui born of the mistress of a house Hû . . . The name Hui belongs
almost exclusively to the XVIIIth and XIXth
dynasties. The monument is no doubt Ramesside.

The other objects in the Plate are fragments
of basalt bowls. These were all found on the
north side of the great Temenos.

Most of the antiquities which Mr. Gardner
brought home have passed through my hands,
and there are a few matters to note of importance from the point of view of Egyptian
archaeology.

A large find of good bronzes was made at
Teh el Barûd and secured by him : but of this
I can say little, as the best were kept at Bulaq.
There must have been a considerable variety
of types. Amongst those brought to England
are Osiris Aah (Pl. XV. 14), Amen Râ holding
the scimitar, and several small figures of
persons in the act of offering to deities.

The use of flint in late times is confirmed
by a flake of the ordinary type. We found
several flint instruments and flakes of the
rudest kind at Naukratis in 1885, and at
Nebesheh in 1886, and it seems impossible that
they should have been used either as ceremonial
implements or as amulets after their true use
was forgotten.

---

[8] So apparently on the original.

[9] The passage is very doubtful. The signs resemble

It seems that flint remained as an occasional cheap substitute for metal amongst the poorest down to a very late period.

Some of the pottery brought back is of the thin whitish Saite ware, such as is found at Defeneh. There are also fragments of bronze graters like those from Tel el Yahudîyeh,[1] and two or three small whetstones of the same form as at Defenoh. Most of the pottery from the cemetery seems to be Ptolemaic.

There are two fragments of coarse red pottery with ⟨𓎺 𓈗⟩ alone incised in large and clear semi-hieratic signs. Possibly the following will throw light on this.

There is a fragment of a very small ushabti in powdery bluish paste, yellow on the surface, like the Greek scarabs, and evidently made in the Greek workshops. It is (see Pl. XXIV.) of the ⟨𓏏𓊪𓈖𓏤𓉐𓈖⟩, "priest of Amen, the great lion, the priest of Osiris " . . . . . It is unfortunately much worn. This figure has been intended for a local dignitary. The inscription reminds one of the lion over the nome sign of the Prosopite nome on the stamp. (See below.)

Osiris appears again as Osiris ṭaṭ ⟨𓏏𓄿𓏏𓊽𓊽⟩, on a fragment of a rude "pastophorus" statuette in basalt from Naukratis.

A Greek white paste scarab has the name Rā nefer ka of Shabaka, the first king of the XXVth dynasty. See Pl. XXIV. I do not think that this is contemporary with the king.

The base of a small statue in basalt, probably Ptolemaic, has a long religious inscription, but unfortunately the name and title of the owner are lost.

On Pl. XV. 5 are casts from a stamp of white limestone, the handle of which (not shown) is a globular perforated knob on the centre of the top. The seal at the base is in deep in-

taglio, and represents a bull with its hieroglyphic name ⟨𓊲⟩ in front of it. On the sides are designs marked rudely with shallow cutting. (1) a fox, in front ⟨𓏲⟩; behind, a palm-branch—(2) Two men holding a palm-branch between them—(3) Two seated figures : between them, ⟨𓋹⟩—(4) Hawk (?)-headed sphinx or lion recumbent, over the signs of the nome of southern Sap or Prosopis (?)—(4) and the seal, are doubtless significant, but I do not know how to explain them.

F. Ll. Griffith, *November*, 1887.

Last December I again passed over some of the old ground about Naukratis. The observations that I made relative to the subjects of the foregoing chapter are as follows :—

Kûm el Ḥiṣn.—The sign beneath the cartouche on the throne of I. is clearly ⟨𓌢⟩ not ⟨𓄿⟩. On II., beneath the cartouche of Rameses II., is ⟨𓎛⟩. There are sandals on the feet. On each side of the throne there is an enormous ⟨𓌢⟩. These two monuments are in *soft* sandstone and are rapidly being destroyed. It is clear that they were despatched from Silsileh ? on the occasion of some festival at which the king presided, perhaps that of the god Rā.

The granite statue IV. holds one standard only, in the left hand.

I rather fancy that in Kûm el Ḥiṣn we may see a residence of Rameses II. The pottery in the deeper parts lying *on the sand* appeared to me to be distinctly Ramesside. Thus, at least, there was a great extension in the Ramesside period over new ground. Cf. the name Ramsîs in the neighbourhood.

The temple was dedicated to Sekhet Hathor, mistress of the (city of) palm-trees. Is there not in Zimrân en nakhl (Z. of the palm) a reminiscence of a sacred palm ?

I think that the nome capital is to be looked for elsewhere.

Kûm el Ḥiṣn is probably the "Tell abu

Samâdeh près de Damanhour " from which the ushabti in the Louvre, E. 6325, is said to have come.

It appears that it was in the neighbourhood of the city of palm-trees that a battle was fought with the Libyans in the reign of Amen-hotep I. (Max Müller, Proc. S.B.A., March, 1888, p. 287).

Kûm Efrin.—As to Kûm Efrin, I can describe it better. It consists of two enclosures. The eastern one is double, with a long street, formerly paved with limestone, running east and west. I should suggest that a temple lies buried at the west end of the street. There is no sebakh dug in that part, but there are many traces of former limekilns. I much doubt the existence of a temple at the eastern end. Little is to be seen there beyond some limestone blocks high up and some massive brick-walls.

It is a place well worth a trial.

The other enclosure is separated from the first by about 200 yards, and is entirely on the sand of the desert.

Neqrâsh.—The block at Neqrâsh shows part of a procession of persons offering products, probably a nome list, but there is nothing of importance in the inscription.

A copy of the hieroglyphic version of the Rosetta stone was found at Naukratis in 1884 and taken to Bulaq; a Greek version must of course have existed there also. We heard in the winter of 1884 that a large inscribed stone had been found in the north-east part of the great Temenos, and taken away.

Mr. Petrie has pointed out to me that the identification of Neqrâsh with Naukratis was proposed as early as 1819 in the French translation of Strabo by Porte du Theil and Cosay, vol. v., p. 373, note. This was a happy guess of theirs. Why did none of the later geographers accept it, instead of absurdly placing Naukratis at Sâ el Hagar and Dessûq?

There is still an important point about the

geography of Naukratis that has not yet been satisfactorily settled, namely, its position with regard to the river. Mr. Petrie, Naukratis I., pp. 3 and 93, invents an ingenious theory that it lay to the west of the Canobic branch, but on the east bank of a canal which entered that branch at no great distance.

The theory is very taking, as the inconsistencies of the geographers can be explained by their confusion of the river with the canal; but it is worth while to consider another solution which seems to me more probable. The Peutingerian map marks a route along the Canobic branch from Memphis towards Alexandria. The line is drawn on the west side of the river, but I believe only because there was an empty space there. It includes Niciu, which was certainly on the east side; so Naukratis may equally well have been on the east, and the route perhaps crossed to the west of the river at that point. There is here no evidence either way.

Ptolemy's evidence is also doubtful, but the inconsistency can be explained. In the text he places Naukratis expressly with the nomes and cities of the east bank, but describes it as on the river on the west (ἀπὸ δύσμων). When the map is plotted and the river drawn in a straight line between the fixed points, Naukratis falls just on the west. This is perhaps the fault of his imperfect mapping system, and it may have led to the insertion of the words ἀπὸ δύσμων and ἀπὸ ἀνατολῶν in this and the next description.

Strabo is our clearest authority, and in his own mind evidently considered Naukratis as on the east bank, as I believe that Ptolemy did also. Meineke's edition, 1853, divides the paragraphs wrongly. The city Menelaus clearly ends the enumeration of places on the western side of the river below Schedia. Of these, I may say that Gynæcopolis (city of women or of wives) may be the same as Anthylla (the produce of which was given as pin-money to the wife of Amasis, and perhaps this was continued to other queens), and Anthylla may perhaps be identified with Denšâl on the west side of the railway, four miles north of Saft el Molûk, where there is a large mound, though nothing early is visible. Momemphis is perhaps the same as Andropolis, and may be placed possibly at Kûm Afrîn.

After Menelaus, Strabo turns to the other side : " And on the left, in the Delta (the Delta lying between the two branches) on the river is Naukratis, and two schoeni from the river Sais," etc. Again, he says that the Greeks founded Naukratis in the nome of Sais.

These descriptions, especially that of the accurate geographer Strabo, are of greater weight than the very imperfect maps and charts of the time, and I rather think that it is not necessary to resort to the canal theory to explain the inconsistencies. I believe that Naukratis lay on the east bank of the Canopic branch (now surviving in the little canal between Nebireh and Kûm Ga'êf), that the gateway of the great enclosure therefore led to the river and not to a canal, and that the difficulties are all due to the vague knowledge of copyists in the middle ages.[1]

Teh el Barûd.—At Teh el Barûd a massive limestone sarcophagus has been found in the mounds west of the station ; numerous chips there show that many others have existed. There is no inscription.

F. Ll. GRIFFITH, *May 10th*, 1888.

---

[1] Mr. Petrie has ably utilized two pieces of evidence besides those that are mentioned above. These are :—the inundation route from Naukratis to Memphis past the pyramids. Herod. ii. 97. Mr. Petrie identifies this with his canal. Doubtless navigable canals branched off at many points.— Secondly, the existence of a broad dry channel east of Teh el Barûd. But this channel is not less than seven or eight miles east of Naukratis, and to identify it with the Canobic branch would magnify the error and confusion in Ptolemy.

CONTENTS OF PLATES.

8. Part of a face in terra-cotta ; good period.

9. Sphinx; terra-cotta.

10. Archaic gorgon in terra-cotta; part of the body as well as the head is represented.

11. Satyr dangling bunch of grapes to amuse a child he carries, the infant Dionysus. Terra-cotta, of fine work. This type is interesting, from its similarity to the position by some suggested for the Hermes of Praxiteles.

12, 13, 14. Amen (bronze); Horus (dark limestone); seated Osiris (bronze); Egyptian figures, from Kum el Teb, now Tch-el-Barud.

XVI.

Selection of objects from the cemetery.

1—5, 8—14. Terra-cotta ornaments from wooden coffins (except 5, which is of white plaster). Early Ptolemaic period.

1—5. Gorgoneia.

6. Minute ornament in form of gorgoneion.

7. Small bronze bell; these usually have iron clappers.

8, 9. Gryphons.

10, 11. Bucrania.

12—14. Rosettes.

15. Miniature amphora, in form of almond.

16. Terra-cotta figures ; child carrying some object.

17. Two bronze implements ; one forked at both ends, perhaps for netting, the other ending in a minute spoon-bowl.

18. Terra-cotta group of Eros and Psyche; this is worked as a relief, only in front, the back being hollow.

19. Askion of peculiar form; hard early ware.

20. Polychrome lecythus, ornamented with gold and relief work. The subject is interesting ; Eros mounting a ladder with a censer, between two female figures.

XVII.

1. Bone cylinder, ornamented with circles.

2. Small archaic head, of limestone.

3. Caricature, with inscription. A satyr-like head is scratched on the bottom of a vase, and round it is written Ἀπελλαμονεῖον (an adjective formed from a proper name) πιθάκου μίμημ' ἐκνε. Does this mean "the likeness of that ape, Apellamon," or something of the sort ?

4, 6. Two small porcelain figures, representing a flute-player and a man kneeling and holding a shrine, after an Egyptian model.

5. The four sides and the bottom of a limestone seal ; photographed from impressions prepared by Mr. Ready. I am indebted to Mr. F. Ll. Griffith for his help in the following description of the designs. On the bottom, or seal proper, is a bull on a standard with the hieroglyph ga, signifying bull. On one side is a lion, apparently hawk-headed, and beneath it the name of the IVth nome of Lower Egypt, Sắp(?)res Prosopites. The connection of these symbols is not obvious. The other three sides contain designs which are probably mere ornamentation and of no significance. On one side is an animal, perhaps an ichneumon, with the symbol nefer, "beautiful" (often applied to sacred animals) in front of it, and a palm branch above. On another side two male figures hold a palm branch between them. On the fourth, two figures holding some kind of sceptre are seated facing each other, with the symbol of life between them.

7. Bronze ring overlaid with gold, from the cemetery ; it bears an intaglio representing Eros crouching, and holding a wreath on a stick.

8, 9. Two blue paste scarabæi.

10. Flat tray, carved in the form of an ibex, of dark limestone.

11. Head of blue porcelain. This head, which seems to be a portrait of Ptolemaic period, bears a strong resemblance, especially in the treatment of the hair, to that of Berenice II. upon coins, and may even represent

that queen. It is not clear whether this head once formed part of a complete figure.

12. Vase of red glazed ware, late but good work; it represents the type of Aphrodite Anadyomene.

13. Archaic head, of hard limestone. This head is peculiar in type; the hooked nose is very unlike that of a Greek archaic head, and may, perhaps, be due to Egyptian influence. It is barely possible, however, that this head is not really of early date, but an imitation of Ptolemaic period.

XVIII.

Scarabæi; the eight rows at the top are of paste, the three at the bottom of stone.

XIX.

1. Dog couchant, with paws crossed ; in very hard, white stone.

2. Very unusual form of symbolic eye, in soft yellow paste.

3. Situla in hard paste.

4. Ibis in lapis lazuli.

5. Head in soft yellow paste with wreath of flowers, orginally thinly glazed.

6. Seal with name of Seti I., in drab glazed paste.

7. Bulla in sheet gold impressed.

8. Head of ibex in schist. The work of this is most exquisite; the delicate curves of the surface being perfectly rendered.

9. Scarabæoid, roughly rounded on back, in obsidian.

10. Gold earring, hook broken.

11. Pendant in blue paste.

12. Seal impression in clay from a papyrus.

13. Seal impression in clay, inscribed ΤΑ.

14. Plaque of green glazed paste ; reading "I am the servant of Bast, Ra-user-ma sotep-en-(ra)," apparently referring to Sheshonk III., whose cartouche is written with the feather for Ma, and who was devoted to Bast, being named Si-Bast. This is a very interesting object, such

an inscription being very rare if not unique on an amulet.

15. Head of Hathor, of flat work, in rich blue paste.

16. Fragment of plaque, in soft white paste, formerly glazed ?

(W. M. F. P.)

XX.

Objects left at Bulak by Mr. Petrie in 1885. At the top are inscriptions, transcribed in Chap. VIII. Below is a fragment of a large plate in black and purple and white on a drab ground (type F. b. 4), and the two sides of a large limestone seal.

XXI.

Inscriptions from the temenos of Aphrodite.

XXII.

Inscriptions from elsewhere.

XXIII.

1. Kneeling figure in limestone.

A. Inscription on back pilaster.

B. „ „ lap.

C. „ „ front of base.

2. Limestone tablet from the neighbourhood of Naukratis.

3—6. Portions of basalt bowls with inscriptions round the outside.

(F. Ll. G.)

XXIV.

Rough plan of temple enclosure, Kûm-el Hisn.

Inscriptions on monuments of Rameses II. in the temple area.

I., II. Sandstone groups.

III. Sandstone statue.

IV. Granite statue.

Greek paste scarab with the name of Shabako. Naukratis.

Inscription on Greek paste ushabti. Naukratis.

(F. Ll. G.)

INDEX.

M

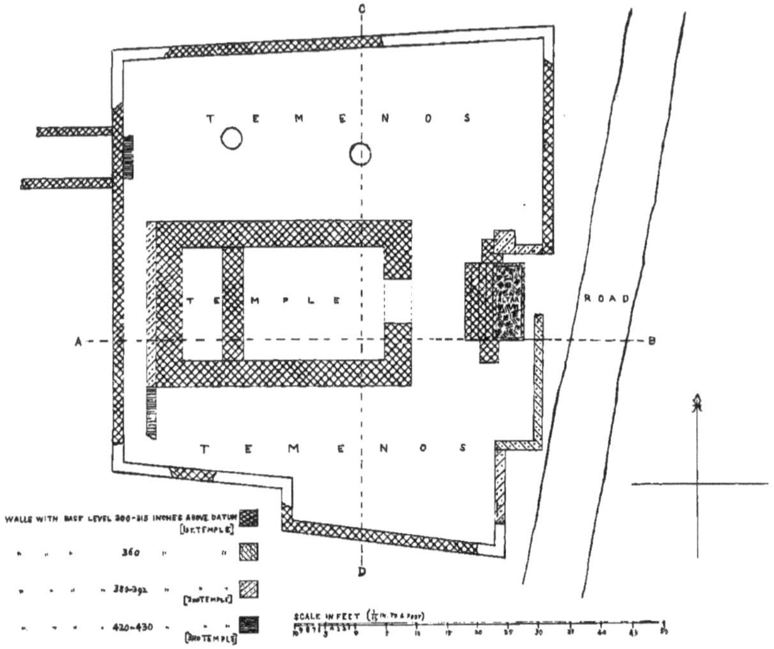

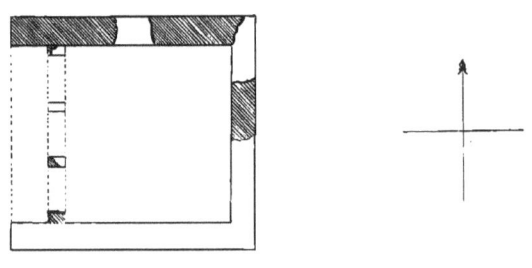

TEMPLE OF DIOSCURI.

E.A.GARDNER DEL.

TEMPLE OF APHRODITE PLAN.

ALTAR

TEMENOS

CELLA

OPISTHODOMOS

WELL 1

WELL 2

TEMENOS

SCALE IN FEET (⅛ IN. = 1 FOOT)

FIRST TEMPLE
SECOND TEMPLE
THIRD TEMPLE

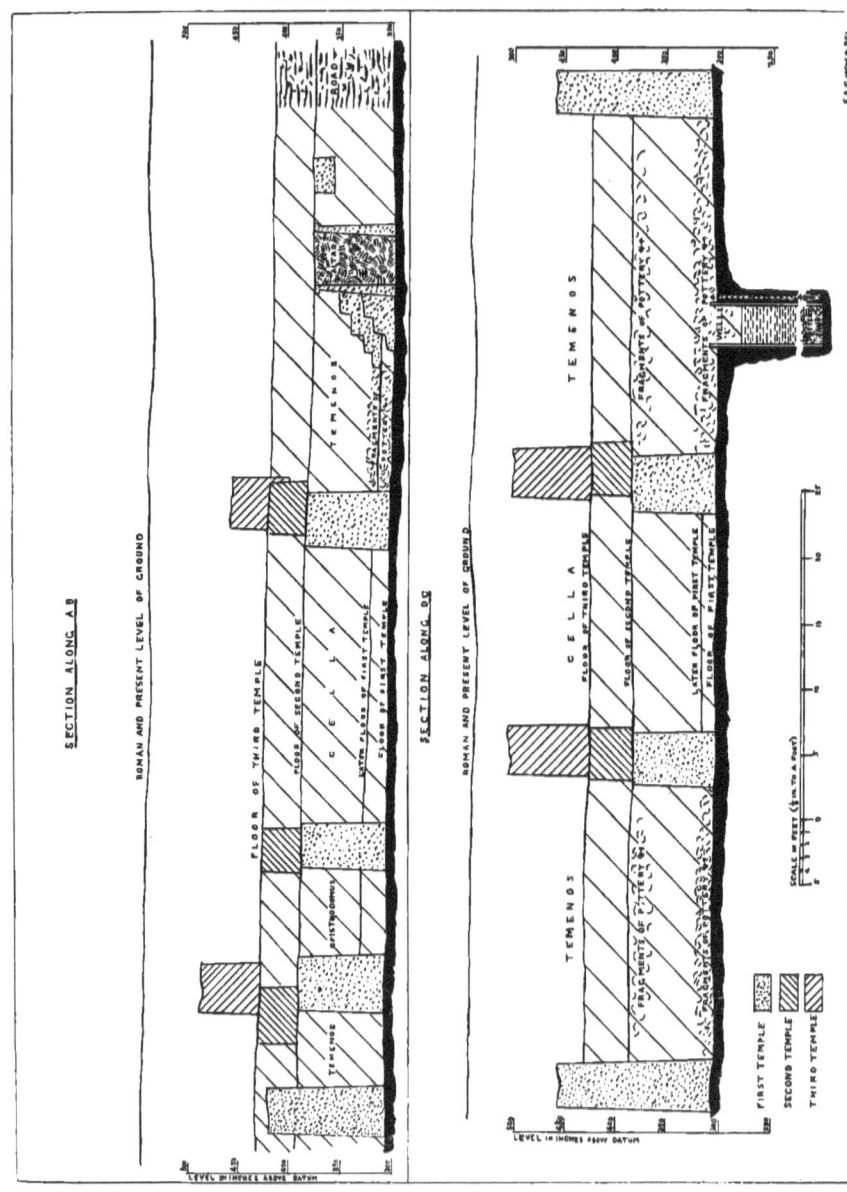

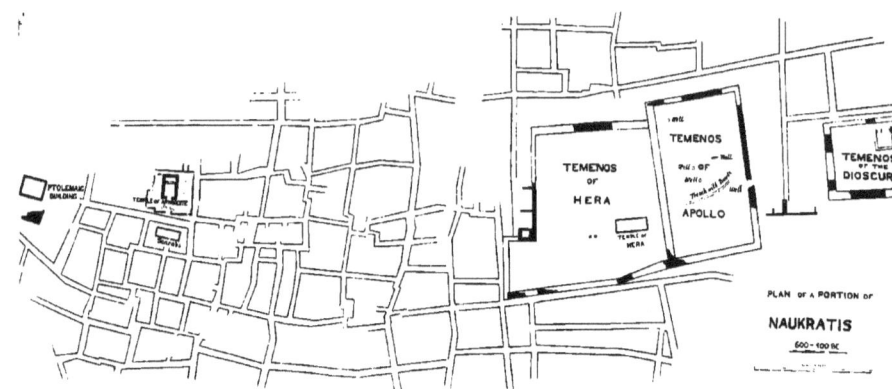

PLAN OF A PORTION OF

NAUKRATIS

600 - 100 BC

1.

2.

3.

4.

5. 6. 7.

1.

2.

1.
2.
3.
4.
5.

1.

2.

1 : 2.

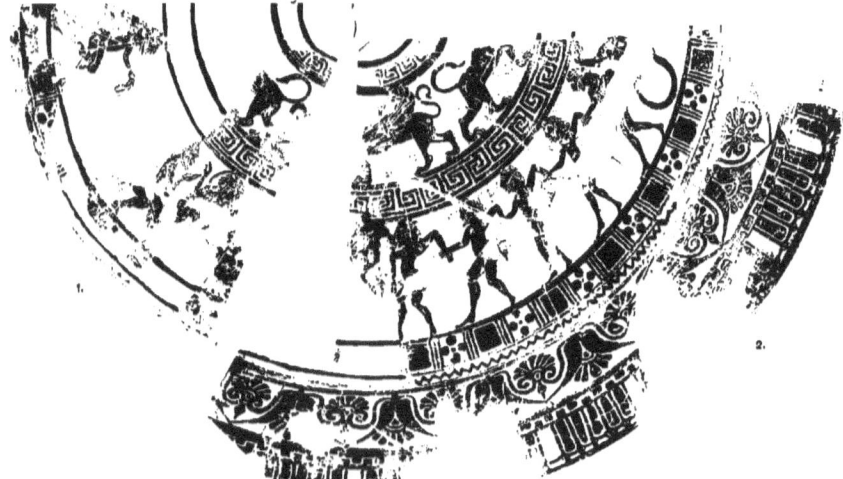

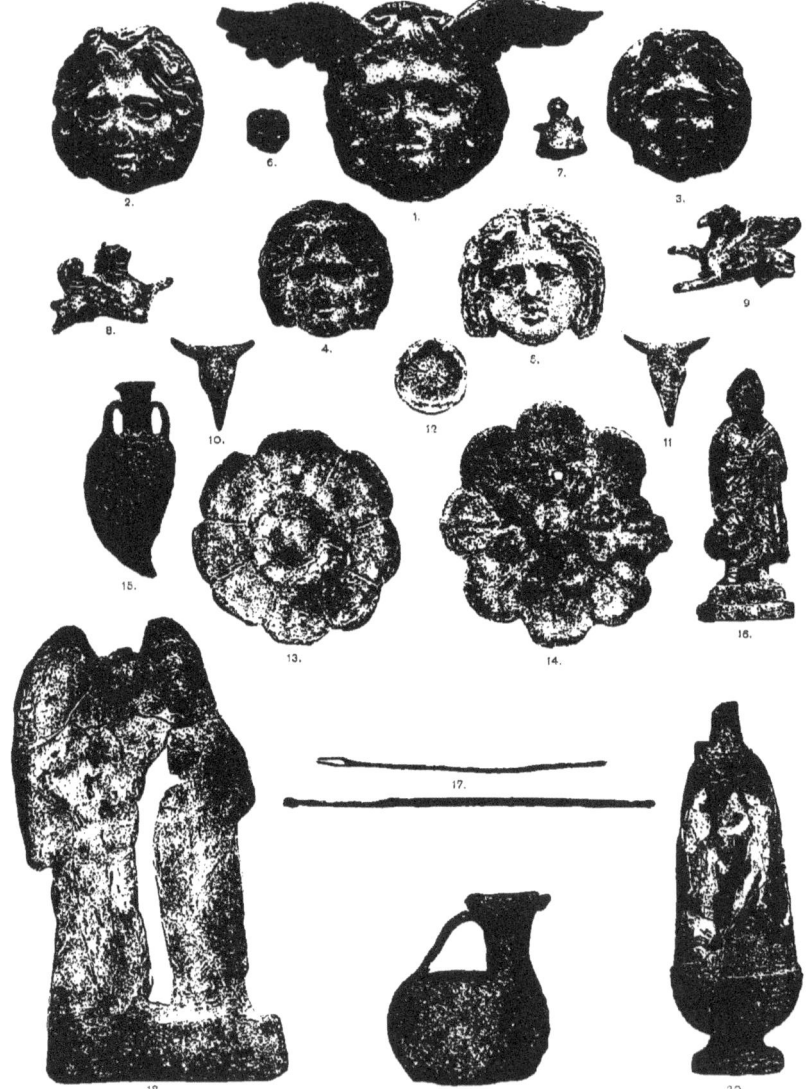

1:1.

VARIOUS SITES.

PL. XVII.

1.
2.
3.
4.
5.
6.
7.
8.
9.
10.
11.
12.
13.

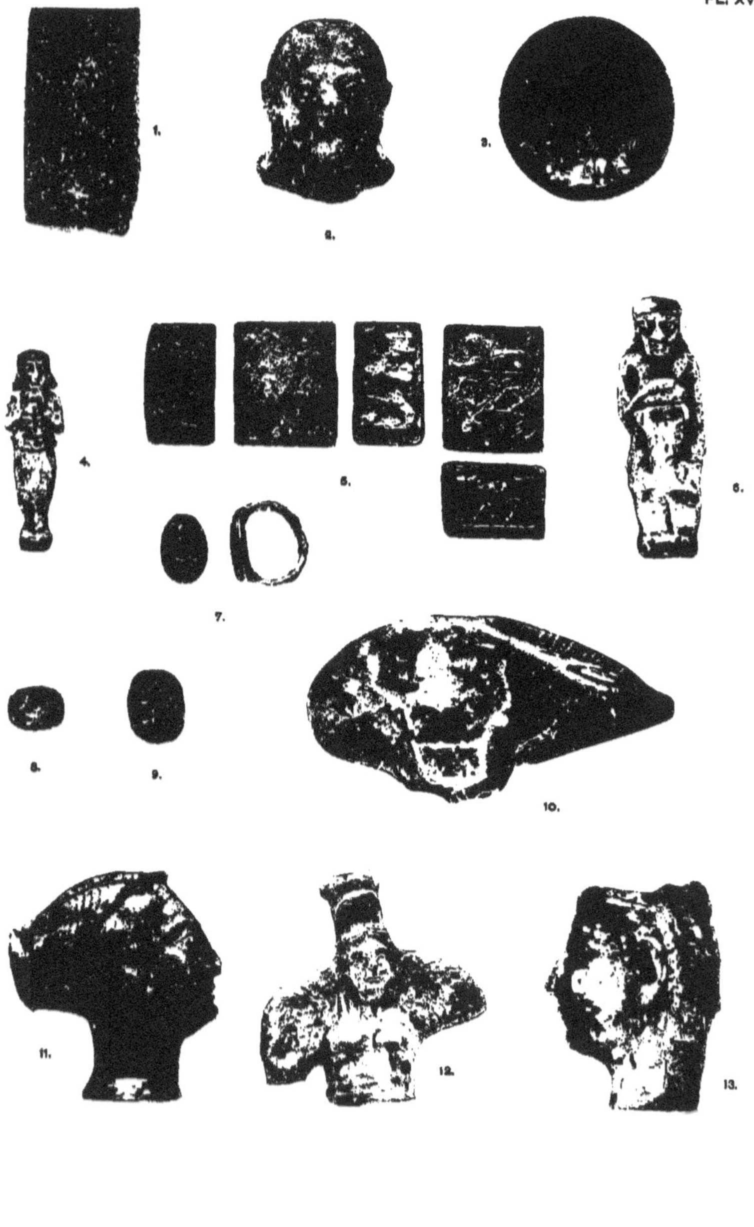

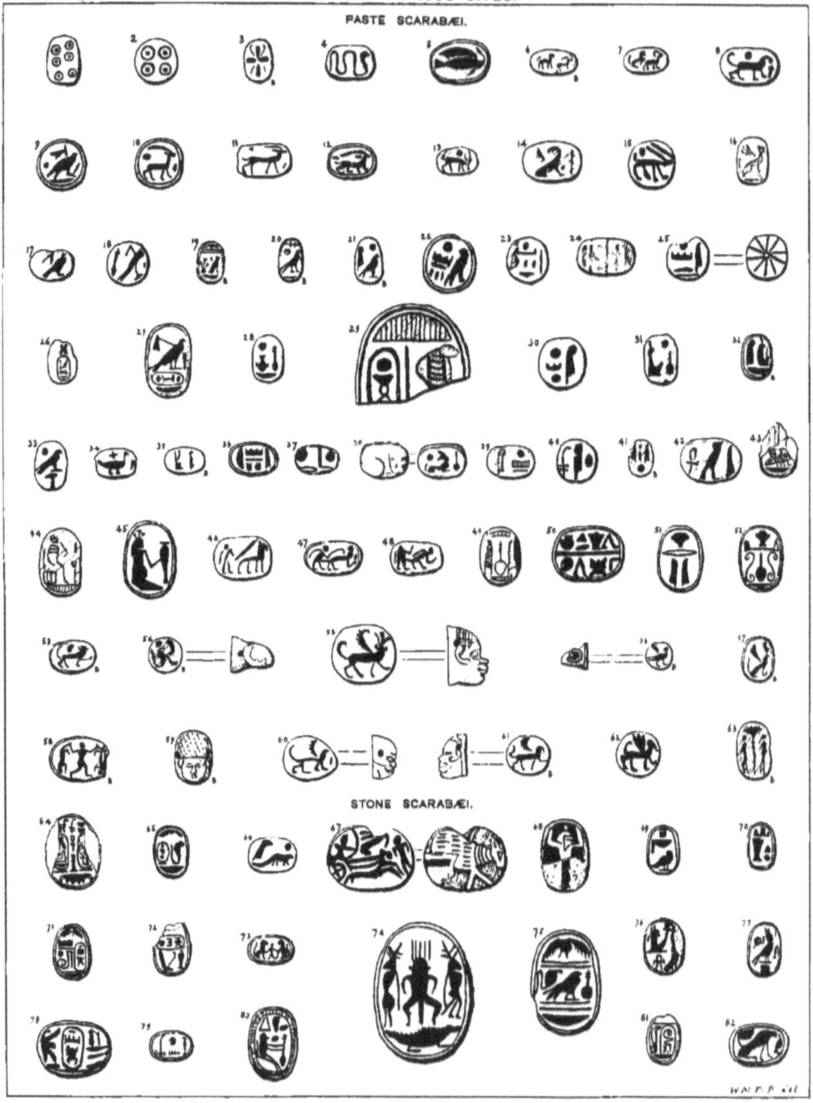
PASTE SCARABÆI.
STONE SCARABÆI.
W.M.F.P. del.

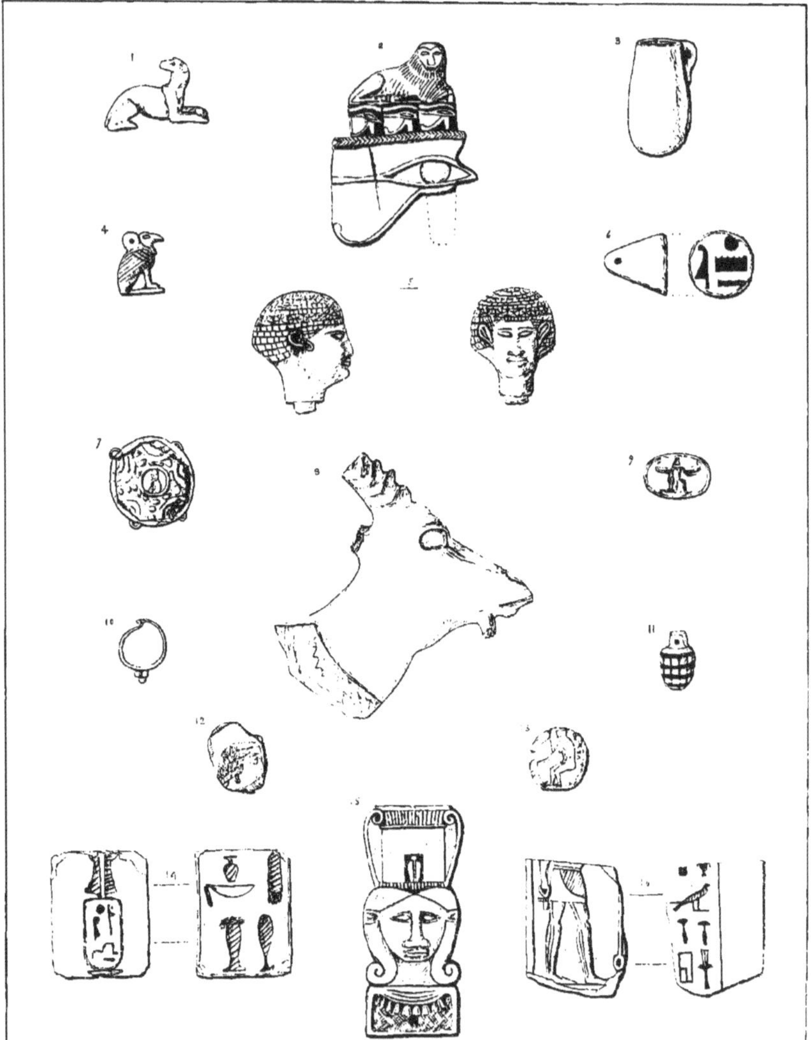

876 ΑΡΜΑΓΟΔΗϹ ΜΑΝΕΘΗΚΕΟΤ
ΤΩΠΟΛΛΩΝΙ

879 ΑΠΟΛΛΠΝΟϹΕΜΙ

880 ΑΠΟΛΛΩ

877 ΠΥΡΟϹΜΕΛΙ

878 ΤΩΠΟΛΛΩΝΟϹ   **881** ΑΠΟΜΩΝΟϹΕΜΙ

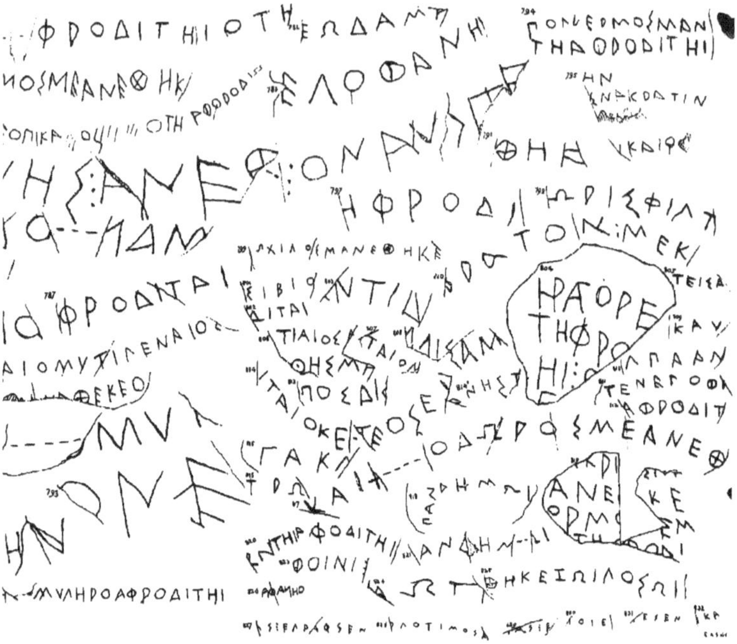

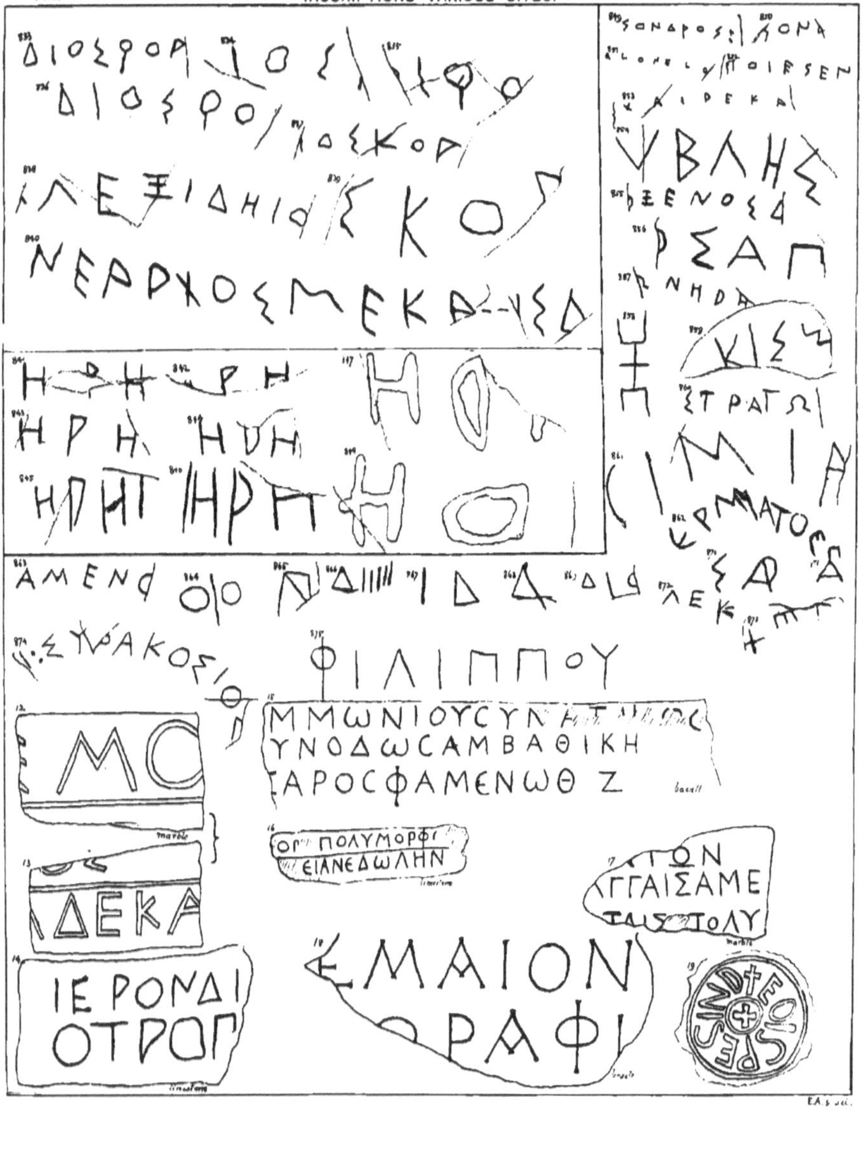

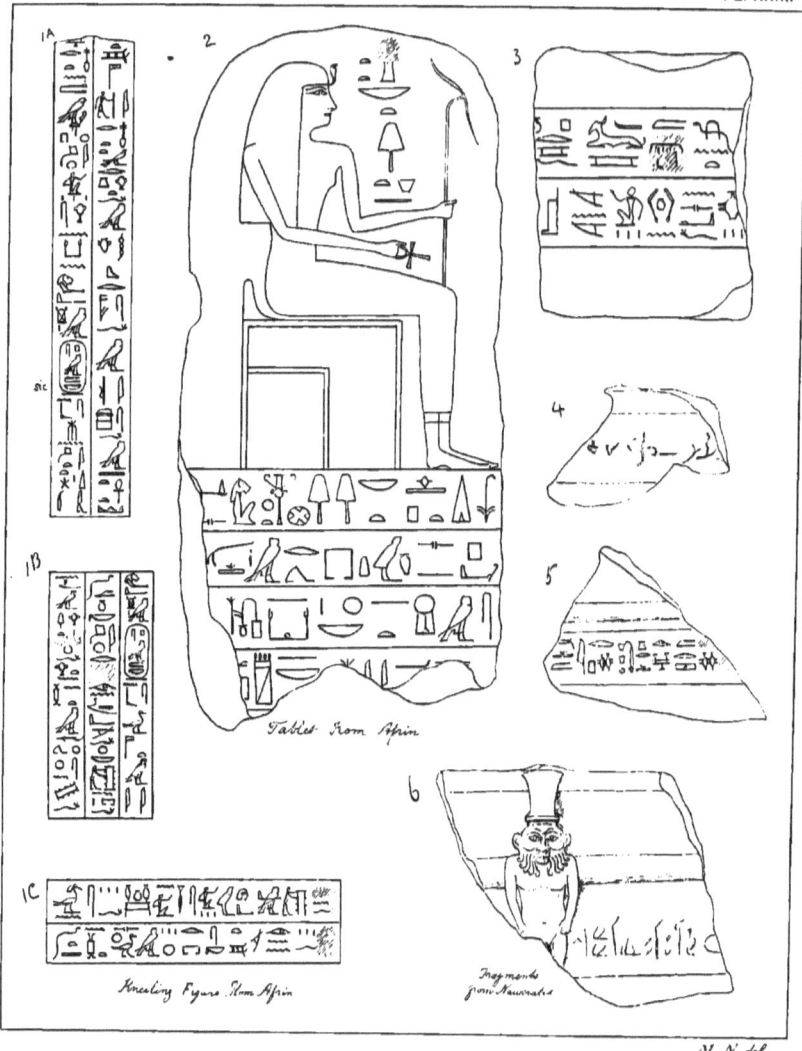

Tablet from Sfin

Kneeling Figure from Sfin

Fragments from Naucratis

M. N. del.

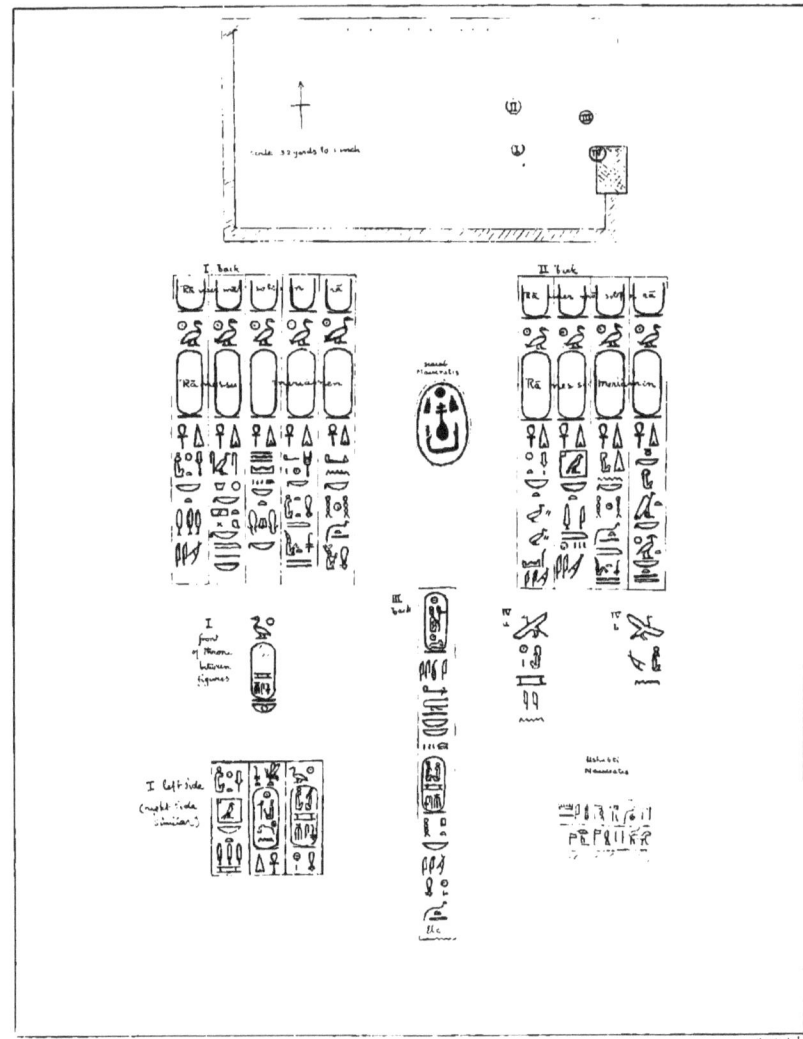